Far from the *World* *We Know*

HARPER BLISS

OTHER HARPER BLISS BOOKS
Life in Bits (with T.B. Markinson)
A Swing at Love (with Caroline Bliss)
No Greater Love than Mine
Once Upon a Princess (with Clare Lydon)
In the Distance There Is Light
The Road to You
Seasons of Love
Release the Stars
Once in a Lifetime
At the Water's Edge
The French Kissing Series
High Rise (The Complete Collection)

THE PINK BEAN SERIES
More Than Words
Crazy for You
Love Without Limits
No Other Love
Water Under Bridges
This Foreign Affair
Everything Between Us
Beneath the Surface
No Strings Attached

For everyone who wrote to me after reading At the Water's Edge.
We are not alone.

1

LAURA

I 've left the past behind, I think, as I flatten the last cardboard box. This one held the few books I brought. I stacked them next to Aunt Milly's on the built-in shelves in her living room—*my* living room. It'll take some time before I can think of this house as mine, especially because it's not—not legally anyway. Aunt Milly's name is on the deed and she's still very much alive, though not so much kicking anymore.

Sweet Aunt Milly, who understood, without me having to say a word, that I needed to leave Chicago, if not for good, then at least for a long time. She's the only person I know in Nelson, Texas. Speaking of which, it's almost time for my daily visit to Aunt Milly at Windsor Oaks, the retirement home she now resides in. I offered—basically insisted—for her to stay in her house. It's surely big enough for the two of us, and I work from home, so I could have taken care of her every need, but she wouldn't have any of it.

"It's time for me to leave as well," she'd said, and, in turn, I had understood her meaning in those few words.

I put the flattened box in the garage with the rest and go in search of my running shoes. Windsor Oaks is in the center of

1

town, about two miles from where I live. Running back and forth doesn't come close to the distances I used to run along Lake Michigan, but it'll do for now. I find myself exhausted after four miles these days. "This could be a result of the severe trauma you suffered," the last doctor I visited in Chicago said. He must have been right. And then, out of nowhere, there are the flashes in my mind again. The ones I'm so powerless against. Blood pooling on the living room carpet and the sound of bone breaking, over and over again. I shake my head and refocus on tying my laces. Running is the only thing that makes that distorted movie in my brain stop.

"ARE you taking care of my spider plant?" Aunt Milly asks, as she does every single day.

In response, I show her a picture I've taken this morning on my phone.

"How do I know you're not showing me the same picture every day?" she asks with a grin.

"You know because I'm your favorite niece and I wouldn't deceive you like that."

"I have no choice but to believe you, but my favorite niece you are." Her face goes blank for an instant. Every time it does, I can't help but wonder whether she's thinking about what I'm thinking about. About the events I asked her not to speak of anymore. That doesn't mean every single second of it doesn't still occupy my mind.

"How was your run?" she asks. "It must be getting hot out there." The temperature in Aunt Milly's room is always exactly the same, no matter the conditions outside, and warm enough for the sweat to keep pearling on my forehead. "This is nothing," Aunt Milly says, then falls silent again.

I wish, for her sake, that I was the kind of person who could

2

make endless chitchat, but that's not me. So we often sink into a companionable silence for minutes on end, me racking my brain for a tidbit of safe information I haven't shared with Aunt Milly yet, and, judging by how her eyelids sometimes droop, my aunt dozing off in her chair. As long as she knows she's not alone, I think, as I always do when I fail to come up with more words.

"Any exciting plans this weekend?" she asks, as her eyelids flutter.

"Tending to your garden." Although garden is a big word for the patch of overgrown grass and weeds at the back of the house. After she broke her hip last year, Aunt Milly wasn't able to take care of it anymore.

"It's your garden now, dear." By the time she gets to the word *dear* her voice has lost its oomph and I can tell she's getting tired. She takes a few seconds to catch her breath. "Why don't you go to Sam's Bar on Saturday? It's not good for you to be on your own all the time." This last statement seems to have zapped the last conversational energy from her body.

"I'm not though, am I?" I give her a kind smile. "I have you." She just nods.

"I'll let you rest now." I push myself out of my chair.

"That's okay, dear. Just stay a little while longer." Aunt Milly closes her eyes.

I sink back into the chair and wait until I hear her breath steady itself and she breaks into a gentle snore. Every day I come here, we perform a different variation of this conversation, and every time, when we reach this bit—contemplative for me, drowsy for her—I think exactly the same thing: being alone is good and I wouldn't want it any other way.

———

AFTER I RETURN HOME and take a quick shower, I stand in front of the fridge and realize it's empty. I quickly push back the memory of how a not properly stocked refrigerator made Tracy feel. I can't help but wonder whether I've become so lax about grocery shopping simply because I can now, then head to the supermarket. Nelson only has one and, when I first arrived, I was amazed by how spotless and brand new it looked. It's not massive, but the aisles are wide and I never feel rushed when I push my cart through them and examine what's on offer.

I don't get out much—Aunt Milly is surely correct about that—so when I do, I like to take my time. I wasn't born a hermit. And a daily run works for me now, but I know its magic will cease to be enough soon. So I make a point of nodding at everyone I encounter, sometimes even throwing in a smile. I'm not out to make friends just yet, but having a chat with someone closer to my age range wouldn't be a bad thing, I guess. I'm just afraid of what might slip out if I let my guard down even a little.

I scan the vegetable aisle, pondering what to make for dinner, when another shopping cart crashes into mine.

"Oh, I'm so very sorry," a woman says, but she doesn't pull her cart back. "I was rushing again, as usual."

"Never mind." I give her a smile so as to reassure her that it's really no big deal.

The woman stares intently at me for a second too long. "You're new in town, aren't you?" she asks. "I've seen you run along Main Street. I have my office there." She paints a big smile on her face and extends a hand. "I'm Tess Douglas, managing editor of *The Nelson Ledger*, which basically means I do everything."

"Nice to meet you. I'm Laura." I barely touch my palm to hers. "And yes, I am new."

Tess flicks a strand of hair away from her shoulders and looks at me again. "Welcome to Nelson," she says. "Are you here to stay? Where did you move from?"

"From Chicago. And I—I might be." I start pulling my cart out of the way, anxious to get back to my shopping and not prolong this conversation.

"Do you work here?" Tess quirks up her eyebrows. She really wants to know everything.

"I'm a freelance graphic designer, so I can work pretty much anywhere."

"Oh!" She clasps a hand over her mouth. "You might just be what I've been looking for, Laura," she exclaims, her voice going all high-pitched.

I should be amused by this comment, but it terrifies me instead. What does this woman want from me? I pull my cart a bit farther away from her to indicate that I want to move on.

"*TNL—The Nelson Ledger*—has been ready for a makeover since I started working for it in 2006… Well, actually, come to think of it, long before that, but I digress. I finally scraped a budget together and I'm ready to start talking about it to people like you."

"I'm very sorry, Tess," I say with a firm voice. "I'm currently not looking for new clients."

Tess's posture deflates a little. Then she inhales, and it's as though the oxygen she sucks in instantly replenishes her bravado. "Maybe you can recommend someone then?"

This woman really will not let up. "Maybe," I mutter.

She reaches into her purse and gets out a business card. "Here. Call or email me if you think of someone… or when you do have time for new clients." She follows up with a wide smile, baring a row of ultra-white teeth.

"Sure." I take the card and, without looking at it, drop it into the side pocket of my jacket. "It was nice meeting you."

"Yes," Tess, who suddenly seems a bit flustered, says. "Take care now." With that, she spins her cart around and heads into the opposite direction.

Full on much, I think, as I follow her with my gaze. She's tall

5

and her full hips sway a little as she walks. Her blond hair comes to well below her shoulders and... her stare unsettled me a little. Perhaps I could have been more polite, but she made me feel so cornered, what with her cart blocking mine—though I could have just turned around.

I refocus my attention on the vegetables to steady myself. I think I'll have sweet potatoes with my dinner tonight.

TESS

"Average height, short dark hair, unfeminine clothes?" Megan asks.

I nod, recalling Laura's jeans and leather jacket. It looked and smelled brand new.

"I've seen her around. I think she's living in Millicent Johnson's house," Megan says.

I shake my head then roll my eyes. "In true Tess Douglas fashion, I put my foot in it again. I came on so strong, she practically ran away from me."

"But your gaydar pinged?" my sister asks.

"Not just pinged, Megs; it shrieked. Loudly."

"And you gave her your card?" Megan keeps repeating everything I said.

Megan's husband, Scott, walks into the den. "What are you gals talking about?"

"Nothing that concerns you, hon," Megan says. "Girl talk."

"All right, all right, I'll make myself scarce then. Jesus." He mock-sighs, gives Megan a quick kiss on the top of the head, and walks into the hallway. "I have a game to watch, anyway," he shouts from around the corner. "I don't have time for your girl talk."

Megan chuckles. "That man."

"He's a good one, Megs," I say.

"Don't I know it." Megan leans against her chair, as if she's pondering all the excellent qualities of her husband and the father of their three children, who are currently at our parents' ranch. Which is also still my home. "But back to you, sis. Judging by the enthusiasm you walked in here with, I gather you'd like to see the mysterious Laura again."

"I would. It's not every day I bump into a fellow lesbian in this town."

"Well, there are Myriam and Isabella," Megan offers, palms wide.

"A fellow lesbian who might be single," I say, though I have no idea whether Laura is single.

"And pleasing to the eye?" Megan asks.

"Extremely," I concur, remembering Laura's blue eyes, smooth, pale skin, and high cheekbones.

"Maybe you should invent a new feature for *The Ledger* in which you interview all new arrivals in Nelson," Megan says.

"That's actually not a bad idea." Hope flares in my stomach. The very reason I'm discussing this with Megan is because I know she can reach the same levels of excitement as I can, and just as easily.

"That was just a joke." Megan cocks her head. "It would be a bit too obvious."

"Oh, and asking her off the bat to redo *The Ledger*'s layout isn't?"

"Well, yes, of course that was too obvious. When will you learn to control yourself, girl?"

"Heck if I know. I'm thirty-nine years old. I'm not going to change overnight, if ever, am I?"

Megan sighs, then smiles. "Christ, I'm happy I no longer have to go through this."

"Rub it in, why don't you."

"I'm just saying… Do you remember how I got my Douglas claws into Scott? I'm the same as you. If it's meant to be, she won't have been put off by your forward ways. You'll get another chance. Make sure you're ready for it."

"How am I supposed to do that?" She didn't even give me her last name, I suddenly think. I can't even google her. Would Laura have googled me? Would she, at least, have visited the website of *The Nelson Ledger*? Or will she just have buried my business card somewhere—or thrown it in the trash, thinking that she doesn't want anything to do with that mad woman she met at the store?

"Take a few deep breaths and keep your cool," Megan says.

"Worst advice ever." I slap my palms onto the table.

"You could go and see her, I guess." Megan shrugs. "It worked for me and Scott."

"Go knock on her door, you mean?" I ask incredulously.

"Why not? What have you got to lose? This could be your soulmate, Tessie." Megan adopts a serious TV newscaster voice. "One cannot play around with these things."

"You're sure she lives in Millicent Johnson's house?" I ask.

"I'm a soccer mom, which means I know everything that goes on in this town," Megan says, her voice devoid of irony. "Between you running *The Ledger* and me spending half the day listening to gossip, the Douglas twins have got Nelson's secrets pretty much covered."

"Apart from Laura's last name and why she would move to this one-horse town," I muse.

"She must be a relative of Millicent's. As far as I know, that house was never on the market."

"Hm, that does make sense. Millicent moved into Windsor

Oaks a few weeks ago." The pieces are starting to come together in my mind.

"Maybe she moved here to help out her aging relative. That would be very noble of her," Megan says.

"There must be a reason." I'm not a journalist as such, but I've always had a good nose for smelling stories—a necessity when trying to come up with news about a town with a population of less than a thousand.

"Let's not jump to conclusions though," Megan insists.

"I'm intrigued." I look into Megan's eyes, which are exactly the same color as my own.

"Here's what you do." My sister is using her serious voice again. "Give it a few days and if you don't hear from her, go to her house. You run *The Ledger*, you can think of an excuse. Tell her you're hunting for a story. Ask her if she'd be interested in introducing herself to the town. Something like that."

"I'll be sure to give that some thought," I say. Then Scott walks in with his mobile phone in his hand.

"Honey, could you tell me why *your* mother is calling *my* phone to ask when we'll be there for dinner?"

"Simple, hon," Megan replies. "I'm talking to my sister and I don't like to be interrupted when I do. I've put my phone on silent."

"Tsss," Scott hisses and hands Megan the phone.

Toby, Max, and little Emma all come running toward me as though they haven't seen me in a month when I pull in to the driveway of the ranch. I quickly get out of the car and hug Emma. The boys are just excited about my arrival, not so much about me actually being there.

"Auntie Tess, I made you a cake," Emma says. "Apple and vanilla."

Before I get the chance to reply, Max, now five and the middle child, says, "It's not real, Auntie Tess. She made it in her plastic oven."

"It is," Emma shrieks.

"I'm sure it will be wonderful, honey," I say, and hold her a little closer. Toby has already wandered off toward the shed. Scott and Megan arrive and park their car behind mine and, as soon as she gets a whiff of her mom being around, Emma shakes herself free from my hug, and rushes toward Megan.

Fifteen minutes later, we sit down to dinner, which is never a quiet affair with three children at the table. Scott occupies himself with feeding Emma, who's only just turned three, while Megan fusses over the boys.

"How much did grandpa spoil you this afternoon?" she asks Max.

"I do no such thing," our dad says, though we all know it's a lie. He's always sneaking the boys candy when no one's looking, against Megan's explicit request to stop. "And when I do give them something, I make them work for it first. Toby helped me feed the cattle today. He's going to grow up one fine rancher." Dad holds up his hand for Toby to slap a high-five against.

"So will I," Max interjects.

"You will become the star quarterback of the high school football team," Scott says. "You'd better start practicing."

Max sits there beaming, in awe of his dad, the football coach, though he's only been playing soccer so far.

"What will I become?" Emma asks with a small voice.

"Anything you want, my little angel," Mom says. "But as far as I'm concerned, you'd make an excellent President of the United States." It's the exact same thing she used to say to Megan and me when we were little. However after college, which we attended together, both my sister and I couldn't wait to get back to this town everyone always wants to get out of.

We could never stand to be away from Earl and Maura Douglas for too long. Megan even lured Scott here to take a non-prestigious job coaching high school. She never dreamed of starting her family anywhere else but here. And me... I gladly took the opportunity to move back into my old bedroom. I tried moving out once, years ago, to live with a woman in Houston, but not only could I not get used to city life, the relationship didn't exactly meet my expectations either.

So, here I am, still living with my parents on the cusp of 40. I'm not unhappy, but, somewhere deep inside, I do feel a clock ticking. Not a biological one—I'm more than content being an aunt to the three rascals sitting across from me. But I'm so ready for true love, I can practically feel the desire for it pulse in my veins. It's in my breath when I inhale and on the back of my eyelids when I close my eyes at night. That's why, every time I meet an attractive woman I even remotely suspect of being a lesbian, my heart does a crazy pitter-patter. And that's how I know I will go knocking on Laura's door one of these days.

3

LAURA

I glare at my computer screen. At the image that is not coming together. My work has suffered since Tracy's death. Where I used to be able to draw a straight line with just a quick flick of my wrist, when I try now, all I get is a line shaken to the core—like me. I try again with the same result and let my pen drop onto the drawing tablet. But I have no choice but to finish this tonight. The client is waiting. One of the few who genuinely didn't mind my relocation from Chicago to Texas. Whereas it is true that I can work from anywhere, most people like to discuss their artwork with the designer in person before trusting them to actually do the job. My portfolio is suffering.

I sigh with exasperation. My portfolio is not alone. My hand is suffering. My bank account is suffering—though it helps that I live rent-free these days. I should have actually taken the woman from the newspaper up on her offer of work. I cast a quick glance at the card that I've shoved to the side of my desk. If only I were a better businesswoman, better at selling myself and my services—but I'm old-fashioned, and I like to let my work speak for itself.

"Right," I say to no one in particular. I know what to do. Sometimes all I can bear are a simple sketch pad and a real pencil in my hands. I grab them from the desk, my gaze drifting to the business card again—the words *The Nelson Ledger* displayed in a ridiculously out-of-date font—and head for the door. Just outside the house, there's an ancient, massive oak tree where robins tend to flock. If I can draw a live bird, I'll be able to cobble together that illustration of 'an arty kind of lion, very stylized' according to the client's brief.

Just as I'm about to open the door, someone knocks on it. I'm so startled that I drop my pencil and sketch pad on the floor. I quietly pick them up, hoping that whoever's there will go away. There goes my chance for drawing outside. I haven't had any visitors here and I have no earthly idea who it could possibly be. If anything was up with Aunt Milly, someone from Windsor Oaks would call me. Or perhaps it's an old acquaintance of my aunt's who doesn't know she doesn't live here anymore. If so, I'd better help them and point them in the direction of the nursing home.

Come on, Laura, I say to myself inside my head. How bad can this possibly be? This is not Chicago, but a small town where people still come knocking on each other's door. With that, I open the front door.

It's her. The woman from the store.

"Hi, er, Laura. Remember me? Tess," the woman says. She rubs her palms on her ochre pants. "Sorry to bother you at home, but I didn't have any other way of contacting you."

My protective instincts take over immediately and what runs through my head is: don't let her in. Under no circumstances let her through the door. It's stronger than myself. My wounds are still too raw. And how does she even know where I live?

Tess fills in the silence that falls. Her Texan accent is very pronounced when she says, "I was wondering if you'd be interested in a feature in *The Nelson Ledger*. Well, I say feature, but I actually mean just a few sentences introducing yourself and your business." Her gaze drops to my hands. "Oh, were you drawing? A drawing would be an excellent accompaniment to the article."

What is this woman babbling about? And why is she after me? Maybe she knows, I think. Maybe she recognized my face from the news. After all, she runs a local gazette, so it stands to reason she would follow national news as well. I tried to minimize coverage about what happened as much as I could, but reporters will stop at nothing these days. And that's what this woman is. A reporter, out for a scoop.

"No. I'm sorry. I'm really not interested in that," I say, my voice stern—I've worked on my tone of voice a lot since the accident. I can state things firmly now, with real meaning behind them. It helps me feel less powerless.

"Oh." Tess slants her head. "Are you sure? It'd be a good way to get to know some people. We're a real friendly bunch, you know?" She gives me a wide smile that comes across as totally fake.

"I can tell." I start to close the door. "Please don't bother me again." I close the door another inch.

"Please, Laura, wait!" Tess yells. "I'm screwing up again. Going about this all wrong. I'm out here kicking myself, I swear."

It's hard to ignore the pleading tone in her voice, so I re-open the door a fraction. "What do you want from me?" I ask. I glare at her with just my head sticking out from behind the door, using it as my shield.

She inhales deeply, then loudly blows air through her nostrils. "I've just calmed myself down. Permission to start this encounter anew?" She peers at me from under her long lashes.

"Fine." I shrug. I must admit to being a tad amused by her tenacity. There's also this vibe coming off her that I can't describe—like there's something intrinsically harmless about her.

"Here I am trying to make you feel welcome while accomplishing the exact opposite. My deepest apologies," she says. "I usually have my head screwed on my shoulders more firmly." She breaks out into a smile. "No more talk about *The Ledger*, I promise. I guess I just wanted to apologize for cornering you at the store the other day. I have a bit of a, er, forward personality." She stands there grinning, clasping her hands together at the waist. "But despite my screw-up, I enjoyed meeting you the other day. I guess that's all."

"Apology accepted," I say, but make no moves to open the door further.

"Would you like to grab a coffee sometime?" Tess asks with her eyebrows raised. "I can give you all the information you need to know about this town."

I weigh my options, and start to, perhaps, get a whiff of what this is really about. Could she be? And if she is a lesbian like me, should I not run for the nearest hill and avoid her altogether? "Look, Tess," I begin.

She stops me and holds up her hands in supplication. "No need to reply now. Think about it. You have my number." She takes a step back, for which I'm grateful. "Okay?" She can't help being pushy though.

"Yeah. Sure, I'll think about it."

"Thank you." Instead of waving goodbye, she holds one hand up to her ear and makes the universal 'call me' sign. Forward isn't strong enough a word to describe this woman's personality.

I don't close the door immediately, trying to show a modicum of politeness. But I already know that there is no way

I'm going for coffee with Tess Douglas. As a matter of fact, I think I'll get rid of that business card sitting on my desk straight away. What does she think? Because we're both lesbians we must have coffee? What is this? The eighties?

Maybe in Nelson, Texas, it is.

4

TESS

I examine *The Nelson Ledger*'s logo again. Even its off-green color is offensive to me now, after all these years of being forced to look at it. I could just bite the bullet and ask Ivan, the guy who's done all *Ledger* graphics for two decades, to come up with something new and fresh. *Yeah right.* He might be able to come up with something new, but it'll never be fresh. And *The Ledger* needs something fresh. On the website, which I put together myself—teaching myself WordPress in the process—it just looks so off. It makes *TNL* look so hopelessly old-fashioned.

I've tried my hand at designing a new house style myself, but I had to admit defeat depressingly quickly. I don't have the skill for it. I just know what's wrong and what will work. I can dream up a concept—I have many written down in a stashed-away notebook—but I can't bring it into reality myself. I need an artist for that.

The thumping of running footsteps outside pulls me out of my dreams for a new *Ledger* logo. The sound immediately makes my heartbeat pick up speed. Could it be her? It's been more than a week since I made a fool of myself outside of

Laura's front door, which, I have concluded, was so ghastly it made her change her running route so as not to have to pass by my office anymore.

I rush out of my chair and pull the front door open. It's her. "Laura," I yell, without giving it any further thought.

She's a few houses farther already, but she stops and turns around.

"Hey." I wave. I shouldn't be so happy to catch a glimpse of her, I think. I'm like a puppy whose owner has returned after weeks of absence.

"Hi," Laura says while catching her breath, then jogs in my direction. She's dressed in a tiny pair of running shorts—the professional kind, I think—and a loose fitting, faded t-shirt.

"Have you thought about my humble invitation to share a cup of coffee with me?" She must think I'm shameless for not knowing when to stop, but, gosh dang, I'm going to keep on trying with her.

"I have." Laura gives me a subtle smile. "I've even visited *The Nelson Ledger*'s website, and I see what you mean."

My heart whoops inside my chest. I really should tone it down. What is wrong with me? Though I know exactly what's wrong with me. It's been far too long since I last met someone who as much as sparked my interest. "You have?" My voice comes out like a jubilant cheer. "Do you have time to meet sometime this week?" I point at the coffee shop across the street. "Mary in there brews the most excellent cup of coffee."

"If she brews tea as well, I could be persuaded." Laura still stands more than an arm's length away from me.

I chuckle. "Of course. Any kind you like."

"Oh really? Does she have Yunnan pu-ehr?" Laura asks.

I burst out in too exuberant laughter. "I honestly haven't a clue."

"How about tomorrow before lunch? Say eleven?" Laura asks.

"I'll be there with bells on." I can't make my lips stop smiling.

"Okay. See you then." Laura gives a quick nod, turns around, and starts running again. She has a graceful stride, as though she's floating over the sidewalk. I do wonder what made her change her mind.

As soon as I go inside I call Megan. Before she can even say hello, I blurt out, "I have a coffee date with Laura tomorrow at eleven."

"That's great news, sis," Megan says. "Good to hear your charm isn't entirely dwarfed by your goofiness." In the background, I hear Toby and Max yelling at each other.

"I'm coming over later, okay? You need to give me detailed instructions on what to wear and how to behave."

"I can pick out a dress for you, hon," Megan says, "but no matter how much I tell you to be calm and collected, I know not even the words of the sibling you shared a womb with are strong enough to actually make you behave that way."

I'M at Mary's Café at ten thirty just so that I can arrange *The Ledger*'s promotional materials in a good way and—ah, who the heck am I kidding? I was falling apart with nerves at the office, kept checking my reflection in the mirror, and couldn't keep my eyes off my watch. As luck would have it, I actually had a meeting scheduled this morning with a freelancer who regularly contributes articles to *The Ledger* about the surrounding towns, but I was quick to postpone that.

Now I sit here drinking too much coffee, and I'm already such a naturally hyped-up person. Megan told me to take at least five deep breaths—in through the nose, out through the mouth—before meeting Laura, so I do that. "Don't think about anything," Megan said. "Focus only on your breathing." I try but find it to be the worst advice ever. As I inhale and exhale deeply, I find it impossible to clear my mind of thoughts. There's always something jumping in. A promise I made to call back the mayor's secretary about a feature. Something Megan said years ago about identical twins with identity issues. The tiny smile on Laura's face when she agreed to meet me here.

"Are you feeling unwell?" A voice comes from behind me. "Your breathing seems labored."

I nearly jump out of my seat, that's how much Laura's voice startles me. She's at least fifteen minutes early. "I was, er, meditating," I quickly say, hoping my cheeks won't flush bright red.

"Good for you," Laura says. I don't have to remember the smile she shot me yesterday because I'm looking straight at it. "I'm going to get a cup of tea. Can I get you anything?"

"Sure. I could do with another cappuccino. Double shot. Mary knows." My self-confidence is returning and I'm able to grin widely at Laura.

She nods and heads to the counter. She's dressed in a pair of jeans, a pristine white t-shirt of the type you can get at any chain store for under $5, and that brand new leather jacket I saw her wearing at the supermarket. She didn't dress up then. Maybe she doesn't do dressing up. I've certainly met a lesbian or two who refuse to cater to the male gaze by doing so and who consider wearing anything else than jeans a compromise they're unwilling to make.

"Mary said she'll bring our beverages right over." Laura sits next to me. "Do you meditate often? It's part of my morning ritual these days. I find it a great help."

"No... My sister told me to take a few deep breaths to curb the worst of my full-on ways," I blurt, as I mentally kick myself for never getting the hang of weighing my words before speaking them.

"Your sister? Does she tell you that before every meeting?" Laura asks.

Our eyes meet and I burst into a nervous giggle. Then I shake my head. "No, she doesn't."

"Here you go, ladies." Mary deposits a cup of tea and a cup of coffee on the table. "Enjoy." She winks at me, which doesn't help with keeping myself calm.

"Which kind did you get?" I try to change the subject, because I don't know anything about meditation—though I make a mental note to do some research on the topic later—and I don't want to delve deeper into the reason Megan made me breathe so heavily in public.

"Just green jasmine." Laura holds her cup up to her mouth and blows on the hot liquid.

"Not a coffee girl?"

"Nope. No coffee, no dairy, and no alcohol."

My eyes grow wide, then I decide to counter. "Tea has caffeine too."

"True, but it has a different effect on the body. The double shot you ordered is going to hit you straight away, whereas this cup of tea is going to have a slow, more lingering effect. Plus, green tea has enough nutritional benefits to cancel out the effect of the caffeine." She puts her cup down. "I'm sorry. I didn't mean to lecture you. I guess I'm a little nervous too. This is my first time actually meeting up with someone since I arrived in Nelson."

"When did you arrive?" Inwardly, I sigh with relief that Laura is nervous too.

"About four weeks ago. I helped my aunt move into Windsor Oaks and now I'm living in her old house. I'm slowly clearing it out. I'm the only family she has left."

"That's very nice of you." I sip from my coffee and await the hit to my nervous system Laura predicted earlier.

Laura shrugs. "I needed a change of scenery."

I sense a reluctance to talk more about that and I'm eager to keep the conversation going. "I know I said it before, but welcome to Nelson. There aren't that many of us, but we do love the community spirit. Apart from four years of college in Austin, I've lived here my entire life."

"That's commitment." Laura sinks her teeth into her bottom lip for an instant.

"When someone hassles me about it, I always say I don't need a wife because I'm married to Nelson." I pull my shoulders up. "Works every time."

Laura nods thoughtfully. She begins to say something, closes her mouth, then starts again. "I assume I pinged your gaydar?"

Now my cheeks *do* flush bright red. "A little," I mutter.

"It's okay." She averts her gaze and looks at *The Nelson Ledger* business and greeting cards I brought. "Shall we get down to business?"

"Sure." I'm still a little flustered, and frustrated because I missed an opportunity to get to know her better. But at least I have confirmation that she's a lesbian and that alone is enough to make my stomach flutter. "As you can see, your newly adopted town needs you." I hold up the last issue of *The Ledger*.

No more smiles from Laura. Her expression has gone all business-like. "What exactly are you looking for? Rebranding? A layout overhaul?"

"The works," I say. "A graphic intervention, basically." I try for a chuckle, but get none.

"What's the budget?" Our gazes meet and cling.

Maybe it's a city thing to be so straightforward about money, but here in Nelson, money is always the very last item on any agenda—and usually discussed in hushed tones. "One thousand dollars," I say with great reluctance and a pinch of embarrassment.

"One thousand?" Laura repeats, an edge of incredulity to her voice.

"Yep… and it took me a long time to come up with that." I

try a grin. "But, of course, payment is not only in dollars. You will also get the never-ending gratitude of the inhabitants of this town for saving them from that hideous green round thing they have to look at every week… and an endless supply of green tea, smiles, and friendship from the managing editor."

Laura chuckles and it feels like a tiny victory. "Do you mind me asking how *The Nelson Ledger* makes any money at all?"

"Oh, it doesn't. The weekly paper issue sells for one dollar—any more and I'd have the council on my back. We get a yearly grant from them that barely covers my measly part-time salary, and we have a very small amount of advertising income."

Laura finishes her tea, then looks at me, her lips pursed together. "So you're really in it for the love of Nelson."

"The nail on the head right there." I swell a little with pride.

"I admire that." She looks me in the eyes briefly, then looks away again.

"In my free time, I help out my parents at the ranch, though they're getting older and they're slowing things down. Selling most of their livestock. I love living on the ranch, but the ranch business ain't for me."

"You live with your parents?" Laura can't keep the disbelief out of her voice.

"Er… yes. Never found a compelling reason to move out, I guess." I try to read her face but, unlike her voice, it appears she's very good at keeping it blank.

She glances at *The Ledger*'s logo and, swiftly, asks me a few questions about the type of new logo I'm looking for. We conclude she'll make a few sketches—so I can get a feel for what she does—and she'll get back to me in a few days. Then we'll decide if we can work on this project together officially.

When she's making moves to leave, I ask, "Laura, er, do you mind me asking what made you change your mind? You seemed so reluctant to meet at first and after I didn't hear from you for a week, I honestly believed you'd be avoiding me for the rest of my days."

"You're very persistent." She gathers her bag from the chair next to her and stands. "And the alternative jogging route I tried for a week after your impromptu visit to my house wasn't working out for me. I like to see at least one person when I go for a run."

She doesn't say it as such, but I guess I can summarize Laura's response in one word: loneliness.

I'm also glad my persistence won out in the end.

5

LAURA

When I arrive at Windsor Oaks the next day, to my surprise, there's a woman coming out of the front gate who looks just like Tess, though I can tell it's not Tess. Her hair is styled differently and she has a pair of thick-rimmed glasses on her nose. I must have stared at her a little too long, because she says, "I know it's confusing, but yes, Tess and I are twins." She extends her hand. "I'm Megan and you must be Laura."

Tess's twin knows my name already? Maybe they're the kind of twins who tell each other everything. "In the flesh." I shake her hand briefly, feeling a bit self-conscious about my sweaty palm—and clothes.

"I was just dropping off some artwork the first graders made for the people in the home. Your aunt lives here, doesn't she?" They must be *that* kind of twins I conclude there and then. Their voices are the same as well.

"She does. I'm here for my daily visit."

"I have my youngest in the car so I can't dilly-dally, but it was lovely meeting you, Laura," Megan says and gives me a quick wave.

"You too," I mumble, though I doubt Megan caught it. She's making a mad dash for the SUV parked a few feet away.

"I MIGHT HAVE MADE AN ACQUAINTANCE," I say to Aunt Milly, and it's as though I can see her perk up at receiving this news. She has always been so supportive. When I came out to my family, my evangelical preacher father and his devoted wife decided my 'choice of lifestyle' was not compatible with their beliefs, and they cut me out of their life. Aunt Milly was the only one who accepted and stood by me.

"That's wonderful, Laura. I know you're wary and it will take the time it takes, but I'm glad for you." Aunt Milly is very alert today—no signs of her dozing off just yet.

"Tess Douglas, who apparently has a twin sister called Megan. She runs *The Nelson Ledger*."

"Oh yes. I know the Douglas girls. One of them is married to the high school football coach, which practically makes them royalty in a town like this."

Not Tess, I think, and remember the comment she made about not having a wife. "I'm doing some design work for *The Ledger*, that's how I met Tess."

"Oh." Aunt Milly slaps a palm against her thigh limply. "I remember now. Yes, Tess Douglas. There was a whole brouhaha when she came out years ago. Nelson has had to evolve since then."

It feels wrong to hear this information from somebody else than Tess, but I am glad to know a little more about her.

"We've had another couple move here since then..." She pauses. "I forget their names, but they live on Birch Street."

Gosh, Nelson is beginning to seem like a hotbed of lesbianism. "Good to know it's not just me then."

"It never is, dear. It never is." Aunt Milly sits up straighter. "Before I forget, Laura, can I ask a favor of you?"

"Anything you want." I hope she's not going to ask me to get to know all of Nelson's lesbians better, but that's hardly Aunt Milly's style.

She reaches for a drawer on her left hand side and takes out a closed envelope. "Could you bring this to Mr. Caan, my lawyer. He'll know what to do with it."

I take the envelope from her. It's light as a feather, as though there's no paper inside. "That's very mysterious."

"I'm just like everyone else in that there are a few things I'd rather not talk about. This is one of them."

"Gotcha. I'll take it over first thing tomorrow." I know very well what Aunt Milly doesn't want to talk about, just as I can guess that what she has given me is most likely something to do with her will.

THE NEXT DAY, after delivering Aunt Milly's mysterious envelope to Mr. Caan's office, I walk into Mary's Café for a follow-up meeting with Tess. Because I didn't know how long it was going to take at the lawyer's, I'm early, and I look over the drawings I made as a potential new logo for *The Nelson Ledger*. Because my shaky arm is still acting up, I drew them on my sketch pad rather than designing them directly on the computer. I'll have to show Tess some color swatches, but one thing's for sure: we're getting rid of that vile green.

After Tess ambushed me at my front door, I wanted to stay away from her. So much so that I changed my running route to Windsor Oaks to avoid passing through Main Street—adding more than a mile each way to the distance. Until I realized how silly I was being avoiding a woman who was offering me work. Business first, I told myself. Not only because of the money—

which is turning out to be quite pitiful—but also to adhere to something resembling a normal life.

As long as I make it crystal clear that I'm in no way, shape or form 'on the market', as quickly as possible, I fail to see a valid reason for not doing business with her. After all, as I've learned after ten years as a freelance graphic designer, one client can lead to another and so on. If I want to make Nelson my home, getting work here should be my priority.

"Green tea?"

I easily recognize Tess's voice by now—I don't talk to many people these days. I guess she likes to arrive early. "I'm fine for now." I look up at her and am, again, amazed by how much she and her sister look alike.

She gestures to Mary behind the counter and sits. "Hi there." There's that stare again, not quite gray and not quite green. I try to remember Megan's eye color, but I was too busy recovering from the shock of seeing a Tess clone to notice. "How are you?" Tess looks at the closed folder on the table. "Can't wait to see what you came up with." The enthusiasm in her voice is flattering, but also a bit nerve-racking. There's always the prospect of disappointing a potential client.

"I'm fine." The times I've spoken those words while, inside, I'm all cramped up with fear and doubt. But today is not too bad. Removing myself from the scene of the crime and putting nine hundred miles between myself and Chicago has helped. Plus, I'm on the cusp of nailing a client *and* making a friend. "Though a little confused."

"Why's that?" Tess thanks Mary for the coffee, then focuses her attention on me again. She's wearing her long hair in a loose pony tail today and that maroon blouse looks good on her.

"I met your twin sister at Windsor Oaks yesterday. Talk about a mind trip. You look so much alike."

A quizzical expression crosses Tess's face. "You met

Megan?" Her voice grows high-pitched. "I can't believe she didn't tell me."

"Neither can I." A giggle escapes my throat.

"Why can't *you* believe it?" Tess cocks her head.

"Because, even though I only met your sister briefly, I got the distinct impression that you ladies tell each other everything. I didn't even have to introduce myself." I hold Tess's gaze and immediately feel sorry for her when her cheeks go pink.

"Well, this is a small town and we don't get new inhabitants every day. I may have mentioned you." Tess recovers well.

"Don't worry. I'm flattered." I feel a smile breaking on my lips—a motion I can't seem to control. Perhaps, after all these months of not allowing myself much room for emotions, I'm starting to get back in touch with the human inside of me.

"Thank goodness." Tess's laugh is a little too wild. "I hope my dear sister didn't offend you in any way?"

"We just had a brief chat. There was no time for her to dish the dirt on you." Something in my stomach twinges, alerting me that I'm about to skirt dangerous territory. The territory of flirting. I clear my throat and change my approach—remembering that if Tess makes any move on me, I will need to shut that down instantly. This light banter between us may be a temporary respite from everything I've been through and the pain I carry with me, but it most certainly can't go anywhere. And it mustn't put unattainable ideas into Tess's head.

"Hallelujah." Tess brings her hands together in front of her face in prayer position. "Because that girl can talk."

I swallow the comment I'm about to make about how totally alike they are in every respect, because, in the end, we're here for business first and foremost. "Shall I show you my sketches?" I tap a finger on the folder in front of me.

"Oh, yes, of course." A hint of hesitation has crept into Tess's tone.

I open the folder and spread out three sheets of paper. "I'm

31

having some computer issues, so I drew them by hand. But I was thinking about this color palette." I show her the turquoise tones I chose.

Tess studies the designs in silence for a few minutes, then exclaims, "Oh my goodness, these are amazing." Tess finds my gaze and, for a moment, it looks as though she might hug me. Then she examines my sketches again. "I'm in absolute awe right now."

My turn to blush. "Thank you. I'm so glad you like them."

"Like them? I *love* them! How am I meant to choose between these three?" She glances at me again, this time holding my gaze. I find it hard to look back so I focus on the smattering of freckles on her nose.

"Too much praise, really. Let's not go overboard."

"You must understand, this is a small town in Texas. Maybe people are used to this amount of talent in Chicago, but in Nelson, this is a treat."

Enough now, I want to say. I know I'm pretty good at drawing but the logos I sketched for *The Ledger*—one inspired by the robins I keep seeing here, one a more sophisticated variation on the current simple, round logo, and the last an outlined sketch of the town hall and its neighboring buildings —are not worthy of that much praise. I shuffle uncomfortably in my seat.

"Too much?" Tess draws her lips into a thin line.

I nod and sip from my tea, which has gone tepid.

"Sorry… but you're hired!" Tess holds out her hand. "That is if you're willing to work with me *and* for the proposed fee."

I stare at her hand for a mute instant, then shake it. "Deal."

"Awesome." Tess's fingers linger on mine and I start pulling my hand away. Her glance skitters away from me and she looks at my sketches again. "Can I hold on to these for a few days? I'd like to show them to a few people before I make my decision."

"Of course." Glad that the awkward moment has passed, I

exhale deeply. I could do with some meditating right about now.

"I'm going to draw up a standard contract for the work. Do you have a business card? I'm going to need your full name or the name of your company."

My full name. A surge of panic washes through me. After Tracy died, I quickly changed my last name back from Hunt to Baker—vowing that I would never again take someone else's last name. "There's a business card in the folder behind the drawings. It should have all the information you need."

Tess is the first person I've given my card to since the accident.

6

TESS

I've practiced enormous amounts of patience. I've tried not to overwhelm Laura with too many emails. The only email I've sent her the past few days is one with the contract, though I did consider it a huge missed opportunity not to go over to her house and have her sign it in person. But I've listened to Megan's advice and I've taken it down a gear.

"You have time," Megan said. "She's not going anywhere."

Laura sent the signed contract back and we're now officially in business. As happy as that makes me, it's hardly enough. On the business card she gave me with the sketches, there's also a phone number. I've only looked at it and considered what I'm about to do a thousand times. My patience has run out. I'm calling her.

"Hello?" Laura's voice is hesitant, almost reluctant.

"Hi, Laura. It's Tess."

"Hi." Laura's tone is clipped. Perhaps she's one of those people who don't like talking over the phone—like my dad who, for some reason, never got the hang of telephone etiquette and always hangs up before I can even say goodbye.

I should have prepared this call better. The reason for my

impromptu call to Laura is blinking in big red letters in my mind, but I need to ease into it. "I hope you don't mind me calling out of the blue like this. I was just wondering how things are going."

"Er, with the design, you mean?" She sounds confused now. "We haven't actually discussed that yet and I'm waiting to hear back from you on a final decision about the logo."

"No, no. Gosh, no. It's Sunday, Laura. I would never bother you about those things on a Sunday. I was wondering how *you* are doing."

"Me? Why?" Laura's phone manners are beginning to resemble my dad's more and more.

"Just out of friendly curiosity." The small of my back breaks out into a sweat.

"Just trying to make sense of Aunt Milly's overgrown garden. I don't exactly have a green thumb, what with being a city girl, but it's a challenge I like to take on."

"You're in luck then," I nearly shout. "I was born and raised on a ranch and I know a thing or two about plants. Need some help?"

"No, that's all right. I enjoy figuring things out myself."

It feels like someone just stomped on my foot very hard. "The offer stands for as long as you like," I'm quick to say.

"Was there anything else?" Laura sounds very keen to get back to pulling weeds.

"No, er, I mean yes. I was wondering if you'd like to go out some time. Grab a drink. Have a meal. You know, a bit like a date?" There. I said the D word.

Silence on the other end of the line.

"Look, Tess."

Now it's starting to feel more like a punch to the gut.

"I'm sorry," Laura continues. "You're a great person and I enjoy working with you, but I'm not looking to date."

"That's fine." The bitter sting of rejection leaves a foul taste in my mouth. "Friends?" I ask with a small voice.

"Yes, yes. Of course."

"I'll be in touch soon about the, er, things." I'm starting to stammer so I'd better hang up. "Bye."

I throw my phone onto my bed and stare at it for a long minute, as though the device is to blame for Laura's response.

There's only one remedy for that feeling of complete inadequacy running through me right now. I grab my phone from the pillow and call my sister.

"SHE SAID NO," I explain to Megan. We're at Sam's Bar and we've both ordered margaritas.

"You can't let it defeat you, sis. If you really like her, you need to give her time."

"But time for what?" I eagerly sip from my drink.

"It could be anything. You don't know her that well. She could have left Chicago to run from a broken relationship. These things take time."

"I know," I groan. "I just… was so excited about her moving here. I had it all figured out in my head already."

"I know what you need, Tessie." Megan looks at me intently. "You need an afternoon with your niece and nephews, say tomorrow after school until about nine?"

"What?" I thump Megan in the hip with a full fist. "I'm sitting here pouring my heart out to you and you're asking me to babysit?"

"I was going to ask you anyway and I wanted to get it out before you had too many of these." She holds up her cocktail glass and clinks it against mine.

"You know I'll do it. I don't have anything better to do with my free time."

"You can stop feeling sorry for yourself now," Megan says. "It's not as though you'll never see her again. You'll be working together on the much-needed and anticipated rejuvenation of *The Ledger*. Use that time to get to know her better. Do it stealthily."

"It's just that, the last time we met, I really thought we had a bit of a vibe going on between us. Some light and flirty banter. God, I enjoyed that so much. It was just so nice to talk to another lesbian. It's hard to explain, but when you never get to do that, and then you do... it just made me feel all warm inside."

"I can arrange for Myriam and Isabella to come over for dinner," Megan says earnestly.

"No. God no. I don't want a double dose of happy coupledom rubbed in my face. Them *and* you and Coach." I take a few big gulps from my drink. "What's the big occasion tomorrow evening anyway?"

Megan pulls up her shoulders. "I don't know. Scott just said, 'Get rid of our spawn, I'm taking you somewhere.'"

"Ugh, that guy." I roll my eyes at Megan.

"I know, he's the worst." Megan sits there smiling broadly.

"I'm just so ready for something to happen. I'm ready to fall in love again. I mistakenly believed Laura would be a good candidate, but, well, I guess I'm on track to become Nelson's lesbian spinster."

"Oh stop it. You're a Douglas, Tess. I won't have that kind of talk." Megan mimics Dad's voice.

Despite myself, I chuckle. I like Laura, but at this point, it's really more my ego that got hurt by her refusal. Besides, I'll be seeing her soon enough. *The Ledger* needs her.

7

LAURA

O n Monday, on my way back from Aunt Milly's, I decide to lengthen my run. I need it to clear my head. All morning, my drawing arm was all tremors and hesitation again. If this persists, I'll go broke in a few months. And then there was Tess's phone call yesterday, which kept me up for a large part of the night battling feelings of inadequacy.

When I came here, on the long drive down from Chicago, I truly believed that with every mile I bridged, I was preparing myself to leave the past behind a bit more. I guess I was wrong. Every night, I see her face in my dreams. The look of disbelief on it—her lips stretched into a vexed O—just before her head crashed against the marble coffee table.

I run faster, hoping that a change of pace will also change my thoughts. But Tracy is still a dark cloud hanging over me. Even now, almost nine months after I buried her.

"She deserved it," my friend Rachel said. But nobody deserves that. I make a mental note to call Rachel as soon as I get home. I need a friendly voice to talk to. Because now I fear I might have blown my chances at friendship with Tess.

I couldn't possible go on a date with her. I'm nowhere near

ready to dredge up my past. Questions would come up and all I'd be doing throughout the evening would be finding acceptable ways to dodge normal conversation. Additionally, I can't make myself vulnerable like that. Nor can I sit across from another woman and let her believe she has a chance with me.

I take a left into a street I've never been down before. Two boys are playing clumsily with a football in the front yard of a house. They wave maniacally as I go past. I give them a smile, and it feels so good to smile. To just forget about everything for a brief instant. I slow my pace a little so I can catch my breath. This is a lovely street, I think, when I hear my name being called. I look back and see Tess in the driveway of the house where the boys were playing.

Oh shit. I thought this street would be safe, as there are no ranches on it, nor does it house the office of *The Ledger*.

"Hey." I jog back a few feet, but keep my distance. This really is a small town.

"Meet my two monsters of nephews, Toby and Max." The boys have come running, curiosity shimmering in their eyes. "Their sister Emma is inside taking a nap."

"Hi guys. I'm Laura." I give the boys another wave. There's no doubt they're Megan's children—and Tess's nephews—what with the freckles on their noses and the green specks in their eyes.

"Do you play football?" the youngest one asks.

I giggle at the thought. "I'm afraid I don't."

"Our dad is the coach," the oldest says, his little chest swelling with pride.

"That's awesome." What else am I supposed to say to that?

"He can throw a ball from here all the way to the end of the street," the youngest says.

"Let's not get carried away, Max." Tess pats him on the shoulder. "Go on. Continue your game. I need to speak to Laura for a second."

Obediently, the boys shuffle back to the lawn.

Tess takes a step closer to me. "I'm sorry about asking you out like that. I don't want things to be awkward between us." She looks tired. I spot dark circles under her eyes that I haven't previously seen.

"It's fine." I wave her off. "It's not you, Tess. You're lovely. I'm just…" I'm what? Broken? Damaged goods? "Not ready for any of that."

Tess nods her understanding. "Bad break-up?"

"Something like that."

"You seem parched. Can I offer you a glass of water?" Thankfully, Tess picks up on my reluctance to delve deeper into the topic. "I need to go back into the house in case Emma wakes up."

I hesitate. My normal reaction would be to say no and continue my run. But Tess has been so nice to me, and I feel like I somehow ought to make it up to her for not wanting to go on a date. "Sure. Thanks."

"Come along then."

I follow her into the house.

"I'm on babysitting duty until tonight. Megan and Scott are on a romantic date." Tess checks the baby monitor. "Which means I'll sleep like a log tonight. Children are so exhausting."

"I can imagine." I'm in the open-plan kitchen of what looks like a modest but beautifully decorated house.

Tess pours me some water and hands me a glass. "There you go." This time, neither her gaze nor her fingers linger. It's as though she can barely look me in the eye.

"What does your sister do?"

"She's a stay-at-home mom, which is quite possibly the toughest job on the planet."

"Do you have any other sisters or brothers?" I ask.

"Nope. Just me and Megs. Mom seems to take strange pleasure in telling us how hard it was to give birth to one child and

41

then having to do it all over again immediately. She claims that's why she never wanted to have any more after that ordeal."

"Who's the oldest?" My casual questions seem to relax Tess.

"I was born first, which makes me thirty minutes older—and oh so much wiser—than Megan." She gives a chuckle. "Oh sweet irony." She waves an arm across the room. "Look at all this. Happily married for sixteen years. To the football coach no less—the value of which should not be underestimated in this town. Her own house, as opposed to still living on Mom and Dad's ranch. Three gorgeous children."

Is Tess having a nervous breakdown in front of me? "Are you all right?"

She pulls her lips into a smile but, even though I don't know her that well, it's as if I can see it's not an entirely genuine one. "Yes. Of course. It's a bit early for my midlife crisis. But, you know, when you have a twin, you basically have to resign yourself to being compared to the other your entire life. Guess who always comes out on top?" That smile has turned into a hint of pout.

"It all depends on how you define success in life. Maybe it's different here, but in Chicago I had quite a few friends who were single by choice—and all the happier for it. Same goes for having children. We, as women, are so trained to believe that it's our highest calling in life to procreate, but when you come to think of it, the planet is already seriously overpopulated. All that was automatically assumed a few decades ago just doesn't fly anymore these days." I seem to have gone back into preacher mode. "I'm sorry, I didn't mean to be all heavy-handed."

"That's quite all right. And I really appreciate what you just said."

"Good." I try to find Tess's eyes, but she still refuses to look at me. "When shall we have our next *Ledger* meeting?"

"Some time this week?" Tess leans against the kitchen counter. Then the baby monitor starts producing noise. "Ah, someone's awake."

"I'll leave you to it," I say. "Shoot me an email about the meeting."

Tess nods and starts for a door to her left, while I head for the front door.

The boys are still playing football outside, though their tiny hands barely have a grasp on the ball.

I wave goodbye and try to fall into the easy running rhythm I was in before, but the ground feels heavy underneath my feet and lifting my legs off it seems like much more of a chore than before I stopped.

AFTER I'VE SHOWERED, I call Rachel—the friend I miss the most after moving south.

"How's Texas treating you?" she asks.

"Not too bad." We talk about Aunt Milly's health and the state of the house and then I just blurt it out. "I met someone. She seems eager."

"How about you? Are you eager?" Rachel's voice is dead serious.

"I like her, but, you know."

"No need to mince your words with me, Laura. I know what Tracy did to you. I saw the evidence. And I understand your hesitation. Don't rush into anything before all your wounds have healed."

"Trust me, I won't. But she asked me out and I said no and now everything is a little awkward between us. Which is a shame because it was just starting to feel good to make a new friend."

"You still have friends in Chicago. Never forget that."

43

Who were part of the reason I wanted to leave. "I think about you all the time, Rach," I joke. It's not a lie, but after what happened, it was hard to even face my best friend and lead a normal life. Because Rachel knew everything and it was hard to look that knowledge in the eye and not hate myself more.

"Let me know when I can come down for the weekend. Are you settled in?"

"More or less, though Aunt Milly has a lot of stuff in the house that I don't know what to do with."

"Has she given you permission to throw it out?"

"She has. She has taken all she needs to the home. Apparently, the older you get, the less stuff you need."

"Take my advice, Laura. Get rid of as much as possible and start fresh. Paint the walls. Get new furniture. Make it your home. In a way, you were lucky that you could leave Chicago and that you weren't tied to a job at a company that needs you to clock in every day. Though I greatly hope you come back to Chi-town one day, you should do everything to start a new life in Nelson. A clean slate, like we talked about."

"Come over soon," I say, more neediness audible in my voice than I would like. "It can get a bit lonely out here in the boondocks."

8

TESS

"I have to go, Dad. I have a meeting." My father just shoved a broom in my hands and asked me to sweep the porch.

"Why do you suddenly have so many meetings? You never used to have so many."

"I told you. I'm rebranding *The Ledger*. I'm meeting the woman who's doing all the graphic design work."

"What's wrong with how *The Ledger* looks now? It has looked like that for fifty years and nobody has ever complained. On the contrary, people will surely start fussing if you change everything around."

I sigh. "The reason I want it changed is *because* it's been the same for that long. It's not modern."

"Pff. Who needs modern when you can have familiar?"

"I know you certainly don't." I push the broom back in his hands. "Here. You do it. It's good exercise."

"Good exercise! Says the girl who sits on her butt all day in meetings." Dad runs his fingers through his beard. "Who is this woman, by the way, Tessie? Do you have something to tell your mother and me?"

"She's new in town." I can't help it. I start blushing. Surely my dad will catch on to it and tease me mercilessly.

"Is that right." He leans on the broom. "And let me guess… she's cute?"

"No. Dad. Lay off. It's a professional meeting. It's nothing like that."

"Sure, honey. Go on. Off you go to your professional meeting. Is that why you were ironing your pants for half an hour this morning?"

"I'm leaving." I head inside to grab my bag and strut to my car, not gracing my father with a glance back. That's the thing about living with your parents. They ask too many questions. They can't help it.

I give our border collie, Moby, a quick scratch behind the ears before hopping into my car. Then I'm off to meet Laura.

LAURA'S already sitting at the same table—soon we'll be able to start calling it 'our table'—when I arrive at Mary's. She's dressed in jeans and t-shirt again, which doesn't make her look frumpy at all. On the contrary. Though I do feel a little over-dressed in my silk blouse and pristinely ironed pants.

"I've been meaning to ask you," she begins to say as soon as she sees me. "Do you go to the hairdresser down the road here, or out of town?" She musses a hand through her hair. "My luscious mane is getting too long."

"I can heartily recommend Connie's Salon," Mary chimes in from behind us. She's just bringing Laura's tea. "And I'd say that even if she weren't my sister."

"I concur." I sit down. "I've been getting my hair done at Connie's forever. Not that it requires a lot of hard work." I did spend more than half an hour blow-drying it this morning, however. "The usual," I say to Mary.

"Connie it is then. Do I need to make an appointment?"

"Heavens no. Just walk in." With that, Mary heads off.

"I like your hair like that." Damn it. I hadn't meant to say that. What is wrong with me? One rejection this week wasn't enough?

Laura runs a hand through her hair again and chuckles self-consciously while she does. "I'm so used to keeping it cropped, but with the move, I've had to forego a bit of my own mainte-nance. I at least need to have it cut into shape a bit more."

"Trust me. Nobody here cares what your hair looks like."

"If that's true," Laura asks, "then why does your hair look as though you paid Connie a visit right before coming here?" Her lips curl into a grin.

"There's nothing wrong with a lady sprucing herself up a bit on a Wednesday." I cup my hand over my hair in an exag-gerated fashion.

"Exactly my point." Laura chuckles and it's the best sound I've heard all day—perhaps all week.

After Mary has brought my coffee, I tell Laura I picked the design with the robin as *The Ledger*'s new logo and she looks at it for a long time, not saying anything.

"Did I pick the wrong one?" I look at her over the rim of my cup.

"No, not at all." Laura shakes her right arm a little. "But that one is the most difficult to digitalize and I've been having some issues with my main instrument lately." She waggles the fingers of her right hand. "This one hasn't been cooperating."

"Have you seen a doctor?" I search Laura's face for signs of worry but she seems unperturbed by what she just said. Either that, or she's an excellent actress.

"No. Not yet. It's probably just the stress of the move and adapting to all the changes in my life."

"And what a big change that must be. Moving here from a city like Chicago?" I probe gently.

47

"It's night and day," Laura says. "I grew up in the suburbs, but lived in the inner city since college. I do love the quiet here, though. It's not until I got here that I realized exactly how stressful city life actually is. There's this unstoppable pulse of energy in the air. People all around all of the time. Traffic. Noise. Confined to living in a small space. Compared to that, the quality of life here is so much better."

"In some ways, but on other fronts… pickings are rather slim," I offer. "No movie theatre, no museums, no nightlife, no concerts… and definitely no lesbian bars."

To my relief, Laura laughs. "It's the same everywhere. Most lesbian bars in Chicago closed years ago. And that's in a city of almost three million. Gay bars aplenty, though I hear their number is dwindling as well, but lesbian bars just can't seem to stay afloat."

"It's because we're cheap dates."

"And there's too much on television."

"And the cat isn't going to feed itself," I add, enjoying this moment so much because it tells me we are still friends. The awkwardness of having asked Laura on a date has passed.

We both giggle a little, then Laura looks me straight in the eyes, and says, "I'm going to tell you a secret that may be considered a crime in Nelson, but I think you can help."

"Shoot." I squirm in my seat with anticipation.

"I'm 41 years old and I've never attended a football game in my life. Can you help me fix that?"

I slant my head to the side and open my palms. "You've come to the right person. I'll hook you up, sister. There's a game this Friday…" I expressly don't ask her to come, wanting her to say the words herself.

"Are you going?" Laura asks.

"Scott wouldn't speak to me for a month if I didn't."

"You go to all his games?" Laura's eyes grow a little wider.

"Of course I do. As I said before, when it comes to entertainment, it's slim pickings in this town."

Laura draws her lips into the most adorable pout before she says, "Could I come with you?"

"I'll get us the best seats. You can count on me." Stupidly, I hold up my palm for a high five. Laura stares at it for a stunned instant, then, ever so gently slaps her palm against mine. Dang. I had to go and make things awkward again. But it doesn't matter, because even if this is not an official date, I've just scored myself some more time with Laura. Something inside me sings with excitement. I decide not to push it by asking her to go for a bite before. Small steps. Or, as Megan called it: stealthily is the way to go.

"Thank you so much for agreeing to take my football virginity." The skin around Laura's eyes crinkles as she breaks out in a smile. And it's as though, in that moment, I can see the woman beneath the wall she built around herself.

I like what I see.

"It will be my pleasure."

Next, we refocus our attention on the reason of our meeting. We agree on a color palette for the logo—the shades of turquoise that Laura suggested—and start talking about the layout of the paper issue.

I end up drinking three coffees and am so wired by the end of the meeting that I actually consider asking Laura if I could join her on her daily run. But then I remember the comment Dad made earlier about my physical condition and I reluctantly realize he's right. I don't want to make a fool of myself by collapsing on the side of the road because I'm not able to keep up with her.

There are stakes in this game. I feel it more every time we meet.

9

LAURA

I arrive at the Nelson Cougars stadium and can't find a place to park. Tess wasn't kidding when she said that Nelson takes its football very seriously. The whole town seems to have come out for it.

I manage to find a spot to park my old Honda at the very end of the street leading to the stadium. I guess I should have left home half an hour earlier if I wanted to park closer. Luckily, Tess promised to get us the best seats in the house. I hurry toward the entrance. Most spectators must be inside already because, apart from a group of sullen teenagers, I'm the only one making my way to the stadium. At the entrance, I don't see Tess, so I grab my phone out of my bag and see that I have 6 missed calls from her and an equal amount of messages. I check the side of my phone and see that I forgot to switch it off silent mode—again.

I ignore the messages and quickly call her back.

"Where are you?" she shouts into my ear. A loud roaring noise filters through the phone.

"At the entrance. I thought you said it started at seven?"

"The game starts at seven but the pre-game festivities start half an hour earlier. I'm sorry, I should have told you that. Hold on, I'm coming to get you."

Christ. And all of that for a bunch of teenagers violently bumping into each other to catch a slippery ball. Though I guess I'd better not say that out loud on these premises.

"Hey." Tess looks flushed when she comes out of the gate. She sounds out of breath too. "Come quickly. It's about to begin."

She gives a ticket to a man guarding the entrance and we rush inside. She leads me to a bench all the way in the front where I see Megan, her three kids, and two older people, huddled together.

"Hi Laura," Toby says. Max gives me a wave as well. The girl —I think her name is Emma—sits comfortably in her grandfather's arms and looks funny in a pair of huge headphones to protect her from the mad noise of the crowd. Because this crowd is mad.

"These are my parents," Tess says, "Maura and Earl, and you've met Megan."

"Hi, Laura." Megan sounds exactly the same as Tess again. "Welcome to the home of the Cougars." She chuckles. "These days that just sounds so wrong."

"Why, Mommy?" Max asks.

"Never you mind," Megan says.

I shake Tess's parents' hands. "They're coming on," Toby shouts.

"The boys get very excited on game night. Mainly because they get to stay up way past their bed time," Tess's mom says. "Very nice to meet you, Laura."

A few feet from us, a broad-shouldered but quite short man who's been pacing up and down the field turns to us and gives us a thumbs-up.

"That's my husband," Megan says.

I nod and think they must look so funny together, with him

being a few inches shorter than his wife. Then, as the crowd breaks out into a huge round of applause, I consider the family I'm sitting with. For the longest time, Tracy was the only family I had. Despite my parents still being alive, they might as well have been dead to me for fifteen years. And I to them, I presume.

The stadium announcer yells out the name of the visiting team as they make their way onto the field. "Put your hands together for the Darthville Cobras, folks." But the crowd has gone quiet now and, beside me, little Max even makes a booing sound.

"That's not very nice," Tess scolds him. "How would you feel about being booed like that?"

"Auntie Tess is right, Max." Megan pulls him close to her and gives him a quick hug.

"I'm sorry," Max says in a small voice. And that's that.

"You're the one keeping Tessie so busy these days," Tess's father says with a big smirk on his face.

"Leave her alone, Earl." His wife pokes him in the side.

"Hey, I'm holding your only granddaughter here," Earl retorts.

"Don't listen to your father, hon," Maura says.

Tess puts a hand on my shoulder and whispers in my ear. "Don't mind them." I feel myself recoil under her touch, but I hope my jacket is thick enough to keep her from feeling my knee-jerk reaction.

"You have a lovely family," I say. Very accepting, I think, but don't add.

"They're not too bad." Luckily, Tess has removed her hand from my shoulder. "Let's focus on the game now. Do you know how it works?"

"I do know that. You can't live in America and not be force-fed the rules of football. It's next in line after learning the pledge of allegiance."

"You'll get along with my brother-in-law swimmingly," Tess says. "Though he believes kids should learn the rules of football first and the pledge second."

"Ah, to go through life pursuing a passion like that." I look over the players in their tight uniform pants and padded shoulders on the field. The Cougars are in blue, the Cobras in red.

"Imagine what it does to him when the team loses. That's an entire weekend ruined. I always see much more of Megan after a loss," Tess jokes.

Because I was listening to Tess, I missed what happened on the field, but something must have occurred because the crowd suddenly goes wild.

"Go, go, go," Megan yells. The boys are beside themselves and Emma shrieks behind me.

"Touchdown Cougars," the announcer says. "What an excellent start to the evening."

Tess is jumping up and down next to me, her hands thrown in the air. I must admit, I feel the adrenaline rush through me as well. Rooting for a winning team is the most fun I've had in ages.

"Go Cougars," Earl yells from behind me, and it makes me break out in laughter again. I've only been here ten minutes and I'm already beginning to understand why my country is so addicted to this sport. It's the emotion we get to unleash in these stands. All the things we need to keep inside during the week, we can let out during the game and the excitement it incites.

"Come on, Jason," Megan shouts. "Kick it through, baby."

All these grown people are getting completely beside themselves because a young man is about to kick a football. It's astounding.

Jason gets the extra point and everyone goes wild again. Tess does as well and, in the process, grabs my upper arm with both her hands and starts shaking.

"Sorry," she says, after she's let go. "Got a little carried away there."

I turn to her and look into her elated face. "I get it," I say. And I do. In a way it reminds me of Sunday mornings in church before I was a teenager. The congregation would come out en masse, all primped up for the occasion, and would just let go of any inhibitions as they sang hymns. While I wonder where this need to lose ourselves like this comes from, I turn to look behind me. There's not a person I can see who hasn't got a huge smile plastered across their face. What can I possibly have against football after witnessing this?

The rest of the evening I watch the Nelson Cougars take two touchdowns, while they score three more themselves, making it a clear win for the home team.

After celebrating loudly for almost thirty minutes, the crowd starts dissipating. The coach comes over to give his wife a celebratory kiss and his kids a hug.

"Bedtime for you now," he says to the kids. I now get what Tess said to me the other day. The five of them look like the picture-perfect family.

The grandparents, children, and Megan quickly say their goodbyes because Emma has already fallen asleep on Earl's arm. Then it's just me and Tess again.

"That was so much fun."

Tess's cheeks are flushed and she has a happy, healthy glow about her. A glow I rarely see on someone in the city.

"Wanna come again next time?"

"Yes, please."

"We'll make a Cougars fan out of you yet."

"You just might." I shuffle my weight around a bit. I know that if I go home I'll be too wired to sleep. "Want to go for a drink?"

"Sure," Tess says, a big grin spreading on her face. "I know just the place."

10

TESS

"You might have seen that Nelson has two bars," I explain to Laura. "Sam's Bar, where everyone else is right now, celebrating and getting drunk and rowdy." I wave my arm across the room. "And this fine, more uptown establishment. And yes, before you say anything, for Nelson, this is uptown." I nod my head solemnly. "I thought you would prefer this place to end your Friday night with."

"You thought correctly." Laura stares into my eyes for an instant.

We order a glass of red wine and a virgin mojito and after the drinks have arrived and we both have a full glass in front of us, Laura says, "Your family is wonderful."

"They're a hard bunch to get away from and therefore are the reason I'm stuck in this town." Even I can hear the smile in my voice. "But yeah, I love them to pieces."

"You're lucky." Laura stares into her non-alcoholic drink.

"What about your family?" At this point, I think it's a fair enough question, seeing that Laura just met mine.

"Classic story of Evangelical Christians losing the most

important part of their Christianity when their daughter comes out as a lesbian."

"Oh shit. Really? Do you see them?"

"Never. They claim I have broken their hearts. And Jesus's." Laura sighs. "The amount of hearts a lesbian telling the truth can break. It's astounding." She utters an uncomfortable laugh.

"I'm so sorry for you, Laura. That's horrible."

"It is what it is. I'm in my forties now, so I can see things more clearly. But growing up, and realizing who I was while knowing how much my parents condemned it. That was pretty hard. For the longest time, I thought it best not to tell them at all. But after college and after meeting so many people whose parents accepted them for who they were, I couldn't hold it in anymore. I told them. The rest is history."

Laura's voice is level and matter-of-fact. She sounds as though she dealt with this a long time ago. But it must still hurt.

I shake my head. "I fail to understand how a parent can turn away from their child like that."

"Religion is a powerful motivator. It doesn't help that my father is a preacher. 'How would it look if I accepted this sort of abomination from my own flesh and blood?' he asked me. 'I can't be that sort of hypocrite.'" Laura looks at me. Her face is blank. "They're dead to me." She sips from her drink. "What is the hardest to accept, I guess, is that they created me. As my father said, I am their flesh and blood. It can mess with your self-esteem when you have zero respect for your parents and their choices."

"Laura. No. You mustn't think that way."

"I don't. Not anymore. But part of growing up is giving in to that relentless desire for your parents to be proud of you. I used to pray to God that I would wake up straight the next day. Vowed I'd do anything."

I can't help it. I reach for Laura's hand and cover it with mine. "But look what a beautiful person you've become."

"I'm not," Laura says resolutely and pulls her hand away. "I've done terrible things."

"I'm sure whatever you've done is no match for how poorly they've treated you." I'm a little stung by how violently Laura drew her hand away.

"Tess, please. You don't know anything about me. You just don't know."

The exhilaration of attending the game together and the intimacy we've been sharing over this cozy table is quickly seeping out of me. An unreasonable anger rises within me as well. Fury at Laura's parents for being so cruel and short-sighted. For loving Jesus more than their own daughter. "You can tell me." I deliberately keep my voice low and soothing.

"I can't. Trust me, you do not want to know." Laura sounds like a trapped animal.

If I push a little bit harder, I think I can get her to open up to me. She's fidgeting with a napkin and her glance skitters here and there—never crossing mine—but she's still in her seat and she has told me more tonight than on any other occasion. We're growing closer. This is my chance. "But I do. I do want to know." *I want to know everything there is to know about you. Everything you'll let me.*

Laura hangs her head low, stares at her hands. "It's not—" She's interrupted by the door of the bar opening with a crash and two people stumbling into the place.

"Look, Myriam. It's Tess Douglas. Football royalty!"

Of all the times to run into Myriam and Isabella. I can just stop myself from rolling my eyes at them. Laura was about to open up to me. I know it. That chance has now swiftly come and gone. Myriam and Isabella stagger toward us, obviously inebriated, and they both start pawing me.

"Coach did a great job tonight, Tessie," Myriam murmurs.

"And who have we here?" Isabella butts in. "We're not interrupting are we?"

I have half a mind to tell her that, yes, they are rudely interrupting, but it would be wasted on their drunken minds.

"Hi. I'm Laura. New in town." Laura has pasted a convivial smile on her face and extends her hand to both of them. Isabella just shakes it, but to my horror, Myriam has the audacity to plant a kiss on top of it.

Thankfully, Laura hasn't lost her sense of humor and she laughs off Myriam's silly gesture.

"We're the other lesbians in Nelson," Isabella says.

"Then I guess that makes me the fourth." Laura seems to have perked up. Perhaps she's just glad to have gotten out of an uncomfortable conversation.

"Let's drink to that!" Myriam says. "What are you ladies having?"

"I'm fine," Laura says.

"The one merlot they serve here." I hold up my near-empty glass.

"Then that's what we'll be having as well." Myriam saunters to the bar to order.

"Did you go to the game?" Isabella asks.

"How could I not have? It was Laura's first Cougars game." I resign myself to the fact that my opportunity to learn more about Laura has passed. There will be others. This is one of the perils of small town living. Around every corner awaits someone who knows you and who has something to say to you. Most of the time, I find this a pleasing thought, though not tonight. Nelson is not a big city in which you can disappear and find anonymity. But, I had planned to introduce Laura to Myriam and Isabella. It's actually fun to be able to hang out with them without feeling like the fifth wheel on the wagon.

"Where do you hail from, Laura?" Isabella asks. Myriam has

come back with the drinks and taken a seat around the table with us.

I watch Laura rattle off her spiel of how she ended up in Nelson of all places. She tells them about her aunt, Chicago, the work she's doing for *The Ledger* and her daily runs. I enjoy observing her, the way she makes minute gestures with her hands—which makes me think of what she said about the tremors in her arm when she draws—and scratches her temple when she contemplates a reply to one of Isabella and Myriam's questions. They're really giving her the third degree now. I'm inclined to step in, make them back off a bit, but Laura is a big girl. She can fend for herself.

I look at her sideways. She has the most beautiful blue eyes —so rare in someone with dark hair like hers. She still hasn't had her hair cut. Does that mean she listened to me when I said I liked it like that? I wonder what it is that she thinks is so awful that she can't tell me. I simply can't imagine someone as soft-spoken and gentle-minded as Laura to have done some-thing terrible.

"What do you think, Tess?" Laura asks me.

Our eyes meet and I can tell from the way she's looking at me that she knows I wasn't following the conversation, that this is her way of inviting me to rejoin. And in that instant, be it my imagination or not, I can feel there is something between us. Whether she likes it or not.

11

LAURA

After that evening at the football game and the subsequent drinks, it's as though my life changes, almost overnight. There's barbecue night at Myriam and Isabella's. I have dinner with Coach Ingersley, Megan, and the children. I get my hair cut at Connie's who fills me in on all the local gossip about people I don't know. And Tess and I end up seeing each other almost every other day.

Yet, I manage to avoid coming close to telling her about Tracy like I did that night after the game. If the other two hadn't come in, I don't know what would have happened. If I would have told her or not. I don't even know how I could possibly get those words to cross my lips.

Even to Aunt Milly, whose mental state seems to be worsening by the day, it is clear that I'm becoming happier, more myself again, less worried about keeping my guard up at all times.

Most of all, I enjoy Tess's company. So much so that, these days, when I draw on the computer, my hand only shakes half as much as it did before I attended my first Cougars game.

It's still spring in Texas but the first signs of the summer humidity already hang in the air on the day that Tess asks me to go for a picnic in a spot she hasn't shown me yet.

"Okay," I say, "but only if we run there." My stamina has increased exponentially and after visiting Aunt Milly at Windsor Oaks I've taken up the habit of straying off my habitual path and exploring the outskirts of the town.

"No can do, Baker," Tess says. "I know you don't drink but I'm planning to take an excellent bottle of vino just for little old *moi*. It's not that I don't want to, of course. You must know that I'm dying to demonstrate my excellent fitness levels to you, but someone has to carry the wares. You can run. You'll be nice and sweaty when you arrive. It's a good look on you."

I shake my head at her. "You know what, Tess? A simple no would have sufficed."

"Perhaps, but it's hardly the Douglas way." She shoots me one of her grins—I have noticed that they've become more and more seductive. But she hasn't asked me out anymore, though we go out together plenty. Just not as a couple. Which is, perhaps, not the way Tess wants it, but it suits me just fine.

Tess drives us a few miles out of town, to the middle of nowhere, then stops. "This is it," she says.

"There's nothing here," I reply.

"That's the whole point." She bounds out of the car and grabs the picnic basket from the trunk. "Just you and me and the Texas skyline. How does it compare to Chicago's?"

"So much more impressive." I follow Tess onto a field. "Aren't we trespassing?"

"Nope. This is Douglas land. My land, in fact. I could build a house here if I wanted to." She turns around and looks at me triumphantly.

"Really?"

"Well, I'd need to get permission, of course. I haven't actually looked into it. But one can dream."

"One can."

Tess starts walking again. She lets her gaze drift over the surroundings, as if she's looking for the perfect spot. "Here will do." She takes a few more paces to the right and spreads out the blanket.

"You have excellent taste." I look her over as she distributes the goodies she brought. Bread, made fresh by Earl, who has recently taken up baking as a hobby. The bottle of wine for her. A bottle of San Pellegrino for me. Egg salad. Grapes. Bread and cold cuts.

Once we're both seated, Tess's legs tucked away chastely under a black summer dress with huge white polka dots, and beverages are poured, Tess says, "I just wanted to thank you for brightening up my life. I wasn't unhappy, but you really have done so. I wanted you to know that." She holds up her glass for me to clink mine against.

"Way to get the heavy stuff out of the way." I softly touch my glass against hers.

"That's not heavy. Wait until I start on my speech," she jokes, then sips from her wine. "Gosh, that's good." She glances over. "You really never drink?"

Here come the questions, I think. I also can't picture myself enjoying alcohol ever again after what happened the last time I drank. "I used to and I could surely *use* a drink from time to time to lessen my inhibitions in social situations, but I feel so good since I stopped drinking. A life without hangovers isn't so bad." I chuckle, hoping that my response was light-hearted enough—despite the reason for my not drinking being anything but.

"Is there a specific reason why you stopped?" Tess asks. Over the past few weeks, ever since I almost spilled the beans at that bar, Tess and I have spent a lot of time together, but never in a setting like this. There were always people around, even just Mary at the café. And we've worked hard on *The Ledger*. I've even gotten some calls from local business owners asking me to work my magic on them. Even more so since Tess gave me a free ad in the last issue of *The Ledger*.

I gather she has brought me here, to this idyllic, discreet spot, to find out more about me. I understand the compulsion, but I don't feel like ruining this beautiful afternoon with my life's sob story, so I decide to turn the tables. "Is there a specific reason why you *do* drink?"

"There are many." Tess drinks again and paints an overjoyed expression on her face, then smacks her lips. "Because it's delicious. Because it makes me a little more audacious than I would otherwise be. Because it takes the edge off after a long day. And I guess, also, because it's just how we grow up these days. You hanker for it as a teenager, then you reach the legal drinking age, and there are no more limits."

"Look, Tess, I'm going to be honest with you." I don't want to lie to her, not even a little white lie. "There is a very specific reason why I don't drink anymore, but I'm not ready to talk about that. Is that okay?"

"Very much so. I appreciate your honesty." She has such a carefree air about her, as though no matter what I say, anything would work for her today. Perhaps I read it wrong, and she did only bring me here to enjoy my company, the quiet, and the view.

"Thank you." We fall into an easy silence and I drink in my surroundings. The sun hangs low in the sky, not quite ready to hide behind the horizon just yet, and casts a pale-orange glow over the infinite green around us. "I'm so glad I didn't move to another city," I muse. "It would have been so much easier to move to New York or San Francisco. Easier for work. Easier to remain discreet. Easier for a lot of things, but I would have never even known this existed. There's a purity here. Maybe it's being surrounded by nature. Or just the general, more gentle way of the people I've met here. It's less harsh. Less demanding."

Tess ponders this for a moment. "Small town life comes with its challenges too."

"Everything does." Although, at the moment, I feel entirely unchallenged.

"Have some Douglas bread. Mom is going crazy now that Dad spends so much time in the kitchen. It's safe to say two people have suffered for this bread." She tears off a chunk with her hands and passes me the loaf.

"Can I ask you a question?" I ask while I rip off my own piece of bread. I smell it while I wait for a reply. I've always held off asking Tess too many intimate questions out of fear they would bring up more reciprocal ones.

"Anything." Her mouth is full, which makes me snicker.

"When was your last serious relationship?"

"Serious, huh? When you live here, where there are not many takers, everything always tends to become much more serious than it has to. Because of the distance. I don't know. Doing long-distance always seems to speed things up because there's so much more talking and processing involved. But… to answer your question. The last time I dated someone for longer than a few months was three very long years ago. Her name was Marla and she lived in Conroe, which is a bearable number of miles away." Tess takes a sip of wine and slips a grape into her mouth before continuing. "We met at an LGBT fundraiser event in Houston. Hit it off. Went on a few dates. Started referring to each other as 'partner'. She met my parents. I didn't meet hers because they live in Florida. But, you know, I wouldn't leave Nelson for her, and she didn't want to move here."

"To this metropolis? How dare she?" It doesn't look as though Tess is still cut up about Marla.

"I know, right? Anyway, since then, I've always tried to make it very clear from the beginning that I'm not moving to

Houston or Dallas or Conroe for anyone. I have land in Nelson, for Christ's sake. Why would I leave my land?"

"You'd be crazy to." I reshuffle my legs because they're starting to tingle from sitting in the same position. "That's a big sacrifice to make though."

Tess sticks out her bottom lip and shakes her head. "Not for me. I only have one family. I wouldn't know what I'd do without them. I talk to my sister every single day and I don't go two without seeing her. Maybe it's a twin thing. But I'd miss them too much if I moved away, which, eventually, would taint the relationship. Of course, I do understand that this is one of the main reasons I'm single. I mean, it can't be lack of charm or anything like that, can it?" She flutters her eyelashes.

"It most certainly cannot." I happily concur.

"And the thought of not seeing the kids. And missing a Cougars home game. Nu-uh. My life is here. No matter how limiting that might be."

"No wonder you're so happy I live here now." I hope she takes it as the casual remark that it's meant to be.

"You have no earthly idea." She purses her lips and holds my gaze for an instant.

"I'm glad I met you too. You've made my life in Nelson so much easier and agreeable."

"And I gave you a job that brought in a thousand bucks. Don't forget!"

"And introduced me to Myriam and Isabella," I add.

"Who are dears, really. Dears with big mouths who drink too much, but dears nonetheless."

"I haven't met anyone in this town who even comes close to being timid," I tease. "Or minces their words in the slightest."

"It's the Texas way. What can I say? We live *and* talk large."

"Never in my life could I have imagined that I would ever end up in Texas. In a town the size of a postage stamp. Doing up a house day-by-day. Watching YouTube videos on how to apply wallpaper."

"How many times has my dad offered you to help with that? But no, the lady must prove her independence by suffering through it on her own."

"The lady must. It's important to me to do it on my own. For the sense of completion it will give me once it's done. So I can look at it and say, I did this."

"How's your arm, by the way? All that painting isn't having too bad an effect?" Tess refills her wine glass.

"It only shakes when I draw. It's the strangest thing. I suspect it might not be a purely physical thing. If anything, doing some manual labor helps make it stronger."

"But it's better?"

I'm strangely touched by Tess's concern. "Yes. Quite a bit."

I can almost see her swallow her next question. So I help her out by asking one of my own. "Any other exciting women in your life since Marla?"

Tess stares at me for a second. Is she trying to remember or considering me for that role?

"I had a one-night stand with a woman in Houston. It wasn't very satisfying."

As a joke, I whistle through my teeth. Though, I guess, seeing as Tess didn't really enjoy it, it's a little inappropriate.

"I'm just an old-fashioned gal, you know? Not that crazy about putting out on the first date. I like to introduce them to my momma and poppa first." Tess snickers.

In that moment, I know what I like about her so much. She doesn't take herself seriously at all. Unlike Tracy, who was always very serious about everything—especially herself.

I laugh and let my head fall back, looking up at the sky. "Uh-oh. There comes trouble."

"Is it a cowboy with a gun?" Tess asks, her chin tilted and

the last of the sun catches in her hair, before it's swallowed by a massive black cloud.

"It's a big fat menacing cloud."

"That's the East Texas spring for you." Tess maneuvers herself up. "Best pack up."

"Thank you for this," I say, intently holding her gaze before she starts putting the leftover bread away. "It was great fun."

TESS

"She's driving me crazy, Megs. And she doesn't even know it."

"Tessie, hon, I told you before. Sometimes patience is all you've got." We're sitting on Megan's porch, watching Scott explain to the boys how to run a route.

"But for how much longer?" I know I sound like a petulant child. "For all I know, she may never be ready. I have no clue. We've been spending all this time together, and we have this energy between us, for sure. But I don't really know that much about her. I've told her as much as I can about me—"

"That's 'cause you're an open book. You couldn't keep your mouth shut to save your life."

"That's not the point. I like her. I really really like her. To the point that my first thought when I wake up is whether I will see her today and, if not, how I can make it so that I do."

"Christ. You've got it good, girl."

"I know. A bit more every day. And all I do is wait, wait, wait. For her to make a first move. But she never does. And it's driving me nuts."

"Here." Megan pours me some more wine. "This should help."

"I really shouldn't. I must be over the limit already." But the glass is already touching my lips. I drink and let the cool liquid ease some of my anguish. "Should I tell her how I feel?" I ask my sister.

She inhales deeply, exhales slowly. Admittedly, it's a question that needs some pondering. "Think about the consequences if you do."

"Best case scenario," I sit up a bit straighter, liking where I'm going with this, "she has been waiting for me to make another move." My posture deflates when I think about the worst case scenario. "But, most likely, she'll just blow me off again."

"One way of looking at it is that you're friends now. Is your friendship strong enough to withstand an amorous confession and possible rejection?" Megan plays devil's advocate.

"But the other way of looking at it is whether I'm strong enough to keep on being her pining friend."

"I know it's not your style, but maybe you should start by dropping some subtle hints," Megan offers.

"That's all I do. More often than not, our conversation turns flirty. Not overly so, but enough for me to know that there's something there. That I'm not imagining things. A woman knows, you know? And I know that Laura is not oblivious to my charms. I just know it. I just don't know what to do about it."

"Trust your gut, Tess." Megan lifts her glass. I do the same.

"Maybe I will." I take a nice hefty gulp. "What have I got to lose?"

WHEN I LEAVE Megan and Scott's house after nine, I'm well

past the limit, but the ranch is only a mile away and Megan lets me borrow her bicycle. I plan to cycle straight home until an idea sparks in my head.

I'm a little tipsy, which, I conclude, should give me the exact amount of courage to tell Laura how I feel *and* a cushion to soften the blow if she responds negatively. Here I go, I think, as my hair flaps in the faint evening breeze. Here I go to tell Laura I love her. I start to hum the song. Riding a bicycle along the small town roads like this in the evening, when there's hardly anyone around, reminds me of when I was younger. Still the same streets, still the same town, I muse, as I turn into Laura's street, fervently hoping she'll still have a light on. I hardly think she'll want to be woken up for my news.

A faint yellow glow comes from the front window, so I ring the bell. It takes a while for Laura to come to the door. When she does, her hair is all awry and she's wearing a pair of pajama bottoms and one of her brand new-looking white t-shirts.

"Tess?"

"The one and only," I joke, and realize I might be a little bit more than tipsy. "I hope I didn't wake you."

"I dozed off in front of the TV. What's up? Is something wrong?" Worry washes over Laura's face.

"Not at all. I know it's late, but can I come in, please?"

Laura opens the door and steps aside. "Are you sure you're all right? You look a bit off."

"I just need to tell you something. I've tried… I've really tried to keep it in, but I can't do it any longer." I stumble into the living room.

"Tess, come on. Just sit down for a minute. I'll get you some water." Laura takes me by the arm and leads me to the sofa. Half of it is covered by a bunch of pillows and a crumpled up blanket.

"I don't want water, Laura," I blurt out. "I want you."

Laura ignores what I just said and goes into the kitchen. A

few long seconds later she returns with a tall glass of water in her hands.

"Drink this. I believe you may have had a bit too much." She shoves the glass into my hands and, when our fingers touch, I just want to keep holding on to her.

I take a few reluctant sips, then put it aside. "I've come to tell you something important."

"Tess," Laura crouches next to me, "don't say things you'll regret in the morning." She puts a hand on my knee and it's all I need to bring this home. "How did you get here? I hope you didn't drive," Laura says before I can launch into my love confession.

"I rode a bicycle," I announce triumphantly.

"Good. Why don't you have some more water and I'll drive you home, okay?"

"Laura, listen to me. I came here for a reason."

"So I gathered." Laura pushes herself up from her crouch and moves to the sofa.

I turn a little so I can look her straight in the eyes. This is no time for averted glances.

"We've been having such a good time together. And I don't want to jeopardize our friendship at all. If you say you need more time, then I'll wait, but I just need to know, Laura, please, am I ever going to have a chance with you? Because I want to… you know. I want to date you. I want to be with you. More and more every day. I just need to know." Saying the words out loud has strangely robbed me of my positive energy. Or perhaps it's the look on Laura's face.

"Listen to me." Laura's tone is much more severe than I want it to be. "We're not going to talk about this now. It's late. You're drunk."

"Just tell me. Should I keep my hopes up or not? Because it's hard. Every time we say goodbye, I feel so elated at first… Because I know we are so good together. As friends, yes, I know." I hold up my hand. "But I want to be more than friends. I want you. And maybe that makes me foolish, but frankly, I don't see why it would."

Laura sighs heavily. "Tess, you're babbling. Come on." She gets up. "I promise we will continue this conversation tomorrow. You'll need to come pick up your bike. But now, you need to go home."

Laura towers over me, her face not exactly open and inviting.

"I'm sorry if this is not what you wanted to hear, but I just really needed to say it." I stand up swiftly, only to stagger backward a little when I do.

She catches me by the elbow and takes the opportunity to lead me outside. She holds my arm all the way to her car, while she unlocks it, then gently coaxes me into the passenger seat.

On the drive to the ranch, I've run out of words—the adrenaline of actually telling her worn off. Laura doesn't say anything either. She just pulls in to the driveway. Tells me to stay seated, and walks around the car to open the door for me.

"Good night, Tess," she says. "Stop by tomorrow."

"I will." I flee from her gaze and hurry inside.

LAURA

While Tess showing up on my doorstep was unexpected, the things she said certainly weren't. We've been growing closer, and I've let her in more, let her see more of myself than I wanted to. Because she has that effect on me. When she comes over tomorrow, I won't have a choice. I can't send her away again with the same old excuse that I need more time. I'll need to tell her, so she can move on. I can't keep it to myself forever. When I'm with her, I can already feel it becoming a secret too big to bear for just me. Like a tumor expanding in my gut, conquering more and more healthy tissue. That's what it feels like.

I hardly sleep a wink, but conclude that might not be a bad thing. Looking tired and worn down might make it easier for Tess when I, inevitably, tell her we can't be together the way she wants us to. It's not that I haven't thought about it. I've even allowed myself the frivolity of entertaining the possibility. Which won't make this any easier.

When Tess rings my bell just before noon, a box of donuts in her hand, she says, "I come bearing gifts. I know these won't make up for my appalling, drunken behavior from last night, but it's a good start."

I let her in and take her to the patio at the back of the house. I pour us both some tea and take one of the donuts to be polite, but nerves are tearing up my stomach and there's no way I can actually eat one.

"I'm so sorry, Laura. I'm so ashamed. You have no idea," Tess says. Though her voice sounds chirpy and she delivers the words with confidence, she can barely look me in the eyes.

"It's okay. Like you said last night: it was something that needed to be said."

"You don't owe me any explanations," Tess insists. "Just because I came knocking on your door boiling over with feelings *and* too much wine in my system. It was my bad."

"No, Tess. I think it's important that I answer your question." I stare at my donut—a bear claw. "When you asked me if you should keep your hopes up about us? I think I do owe you an answer to that."

"Is it going to be an answer I don't want to hear?" Tess asks in a small voice.

"I'm afraid so. But I'm going to explain to you why… I can't be with you and then I hope you will understand."

Tess drops her pink-glazed donut on the table and stares ahead. "Okay."

"I haven't told this to anyone and I need you to promise me that what I'm about to say stays between us. I don't want anyone else to know." I inject some harshness into my tone, but by now I know what Tess and her sister are like and I need to be sure.

"I promise." Tess looks at me now.

"The reason I won't be ready for a relationship any time soon, if ever, is because my wife died ten months ago and… I killed her." My stomach is turning to mush and bile rises to the back of my throat. "It was an accident. More like self-defense.

No charges were brought against me, but the fact remains that another human being died because of something I did. And that's something very, very hard to live with."

"Jesus." Tess's mouth has fallen open slightly. "I'm so sorry."

"We'd been married a bit longer than a year," I continue. If I don't get it all out quickly, I fear I'll have to keep it inside of me forever. "I'd gone out with my best friend Rachel. We'd had a few drinks. I came home and Tracy was in one of her moods. She accused me of drinking too much. Of talking about her behind her back with Rachel. And she started coming for me again… fist drawn. A sight I'd seen one too many times by then. Perhaps because I had been drinking, I pushed her away from me before she had the chance to land a blow. It was just a little shove. But she lost her footing, fell, and landed with her head against the coffee table. A solid marble one. Next thing I know, she's not moving and there's a pool of blood on the carpet. The EMT said she would have been dead instantly. As soon as her skull hit the table." I've rambled off the words like they were a story I needed to reproduce for an exam. No emotion in my voice. But tears stream down my face and my hands tremble in my lap. "I killed my wife."

"It was an accident," Tess says, her voice shaking.

"I didn't manage to pick my life back up in Chicago. The only person who knew how abusive Tracy could get was Rachel. Everyone else, her family, our friends, they believed it was a spousal argument gone wrong. Which it was. But they blamed me. And I was… *am* to blame, of course. I did it. I pushed her and caused her death. Which was hard enough to live with already, but all the blame, the hushed voices when I walked into a room, the scolding glances. I had to get away from there. So I came here to start over."

"Jesus, Laura. That must have been hell." Tess plants her elbows on the table. When I shoot her a furtive glance, I can see her eyes are misty too.

"It was. It still is." I wipe some snot from under my nose. "I ran away from everything."

"Laura…" Tess's voice is just a whisper. "She abused you?"

Slowly, I nod. It took a long time before I was able to admit that to myself. "After we got married, something changed. Tracy was always a bit proprietary, a bit possessive and jealous, but she was also funny, terribly sweet at times, unbelievably charming. Dazzling smile. Promising career. She was an architect with one of Chicago's biggest firms. I couldn't believe my luck when she showed interest in me the first time. She wooed me and courted me like there was no tomorrow. I fell for all of it. Until I met the real Tracy Hunt." I manage a small smile. Although the situation isn't very smile-worthy, I feel like if I can smile through this, I can smile through anything. "Then it was too late. I told myself all the regular things after one of her violent outbursts. Classic victim behavior. This was the last time. Next time she lays a finger on me I'll leave. But I never did. I lived a life ruled by fear and every day of being with her, of loving this person who hurt me, chipped away a bit further at my self-esteem. And, you know… I ask myself the question again and again. When I pushed her, what really was my intention?"

"Oh God, Laura. I can't possibly imagine what you've been through, what you're still going through. But please don't blame yourself. You were the victim."

"If only I could say, with my hand on my heart, that, in some of my worst moments, I hadn't wished her dead." I burst into tears again. I haven't cried like this since leaving Chicago.

"It was self-defense." Tess rushes out of her chair. Comes to stand next to me. "It was an accident."

"I know. I know." I've repeated the same words in my head as a mantra for months. "But I still took another person's life. And I have no idea how to ever forgive myself for that."

Tess puts a hand on my arm. "Laura, you are a good person.

No matter who or what you believe you are, I know that much."

I look at Tess's hand on my arm. I inhale deeply, trying to stop the tears. I wipe some of them away with the sleeve of my sweater. "I really think you should find someone else to have a crush on."

Tess's eyes are all kindness, her face radiating nothing but understanding. "Do you think I get to choose?"

"You're wonderful. I thank my lucky stars every day for meeting you. That of all the towns I could have ended up in, I ended up in Nelson. Your town. But I won't ask the impossible of you. I'm the very definition of damaged goods. I have no clue how to ever trust someone, let alone love someone again. You can't wait for me. I'll be your friend. If that's what you want. Though I'll understand if it's too hard. But for the foreseeable future, you and I simply can't be together."

Her grasp on my arm intensifies. "I'm not going anywhere, Laura. Do you really think I would choose not to be friends with you anymore after what you've just confided in me?"

"Not for a second." The smile I give now is more hopeful. "I can be your wing woman when you want to go out some time," I half-joke.

"Oh yeah? And where would we go? Sam's Bar?"

"Why not?" I'm just making conversation to make time pass between what I said before and what I'm saying now. Between the difficult and the mundane. "There's dancing there. You never know who might come along and sweep you off your feet one night."

"Laura." Tess sits on her haunches and brings her face level with mine. "Any time you need me. Any time you want to talk. I'll be there. I really need you to understand that. Forget about what I said last night, okay? I refuse to play the martyr because of how I feel about you. I'm a grown woman. I can take it. We're friends. And I want you to know you can

81

always count on me and I will never expect anything in return."

"I believe you." I feel more tears welling up behind my eyes. These ones are not born from raking up the past, but from looking at the future. From the sliver of hope that Tess's presence in my life represents. In my own way, I've grown to love her too—as best as I can, however stunted that may be. "Thank you."

Tess pushes herself up and plants a tender kiss on the top of my head. A gesture that moves me more than any I've encountered since Tracy died. Tess and I might not be destined for coupledom, but our friendship has definitely breached new ground.

14

TESS

"So Laura doesn't want to be with you, but you don't want
to tell me why?" Megan asks. We're sitting on the front
porch of the ranch. Inside, Dad is reading stories to Emma, and
Mom is making cupcakes with the boys.

"I can't tell you. Please don't make a big deal about it." Truth
be told, I have to bite my tongue. Megan and I have shared all
our secrets since we learned how to speak. Every time something noteworthy has happened to me, my sister has always
been the person I called first. She's my sounding board. My
voice of reason—most of the time. In many ways, my other
half.

"And you've suddenly, magically, accepted that your love for
her won't stand in the way of your friendship?"

"Love for whom?" Mom comes out of the house and starts
butting in.

"Weren't you making cupcakes with Max and Toby?" I ask.

"Can't mix them forever, hon. They're in the oven now."
Mom sits at the table with us and pours herself a glass of iced
tea. "They'll be ready in not too long."

HARPER BLISS

"We were having a private conversation, Mom," Megan says in the whiny voice she used when she was a teenager.

"What are you saying? That in my own house I can't sit down where I please to have some iced tea? Gosh dang. You two are such princesses." She doesn't budge. "It's not as if I don't know who you're talking about. I'm not blind and I'm not deaf. And I think Laura and Tess would make a dashing couple."

"We are not a couple," I repeat. Perhaps if I repeat it often enough—like an endless refrain in my head—I can begin to accept it. "We're just friends."

"Oh really?" Mom is on a roll today. "Because whenever I see the two of you together I could swear you *are* an item. Just my powers of perception. Even your father has noticed. Heck, even Mary asked me about it the other day."

I roll my eyes at her.

"Don't look at me like that, Tessie. You two have been spending so much time together. This is a small town. People talk. That's just how it goes."

"The town can think what it wants. And next time someone asks you, you can tell them we're just friends." I think of poor Laura, trapped in that traumatized mind of hers. Compared to hers, my life might as well have come straight from a storybook. At least I can sit here and have a conversation with my mother, no matter how much it aggravates me at the moment.

First shunned by her parents, then... that.

"I wonder why, honey." Mom gently grabs a tress of my hair and drapes it over my shoulder. "A gorgeous woman like you. You'd think any lesbian new to town would jump at the chance. Is she involved with someone else?"

"I'm sorry, Mom, but that's really none of your business." When you've lived with your parents all your life, boundaries can start to blur.

"Maybe you should try one of those dating apps. Like Tinder or whatever it's called," Megan offers.

"I'm not interested in dating anyone right now. And you can rest assured that, if and when the right woman comes along, you two will be the first to know."

Mom beams me a smile, and I smile back. "I'd better go check on those cupcakes. And on the kitchen before the boys destroy it. I told them to clean up while I sat down for a minute so heaven knows what I'm going to find."

"I'll come help you, Mom." Megan gets up. "My children, my mess, right?"

A line I've slung in Megan's direction many a time. As they go inside, I slip my phone out of my jeans pocket and, for the first time, type Laura's name into Google. Then I erase it, because what am I possibly hoping to find? What she's told me is already so gruesome. I swipe the browser window away and decide that Laura will tell me everything I need to know without me finding things out behind her back. I also resist the urge to google the name Tracy Hunt and find out what she looked like.

Then, for a split second, I consider installing the app Megan talked about, but consider it pointless as long as my head is filled to the brim with Laura.

THE NEXT DAY at the office, I can't stop thinking about Laura. Not only because I constantly see the new logo she designed, but because I can't get her story out of my head. How she must have felt when I went to her house after we first met and asked if she wanted to have a story in *The Ledger*. And after I asked her out on that date. As much as I try to put myself in her position, I can't even begin to imagine what she went through—and is still going through. Now that I know the extent of her grief and pain, she actually comes across as pretty self-composed. And then… in barged Tess Douglas, with her big mouth and country charm.

I go over all the time we've spent together since I accidentally cornered her in the supermarket, five weeks ago already, and consider how not an hour goes by that I don't think about her. While it stings a bit that I have to let my romantic dream for us go—at least for now—my pain is nothing compared to Laura's.

I shut down my computer for the day and, instead of sitting and thinking about Laura, I decide to call her. Might as well. After the last time I rang her doorbell without invitation, and made such a spectacle of myself, I make a point of asking her in advance whether I can stop by. After she agrees—a pleasant note of surprise in her voice—I pick up a couple of salads from the deli and drive over.

More than anything, I want her to know that she's not alone. Not that I can carry her pain for her, but at least I can be there for her. Sometimes, late at night when I can't sleep, and I picture Laura lying alone in her bed, my stomach knots into a tight ball because I can't be there to hug her and tell her everything is going to be okay.

"Taking pity on me?" she asks when she opens the door.

"Just feeding the hungry." She leads me to the patio table overlooking the garden, which is beginning to look properly taken care of.

I don't feel comfortable starting the conversation. I don't want to push her to say anything and figure Laura will talk when she wants to. I also like to believe that just me being here is enough.

"I was able to make a pretty decent drawing directly on my computer today. Things are looking up."

"Glad to hear. What did you draw?"

"A flyer for the upcoming rodeo. Before Billy asked me to design that, I had no idea this sort of thing actually existed."

"Tsk." I shake my head. "You city slickers don't know anything about fine, small-town traditions."

Laura chuckles, then says, "According to the flyer, members of the audience are invited to have a go on the mechanical bull. Are you game?"

I drop my fork and feign indignation. "Am I game? You happen to be looking at the reigning female champion, two years running!"

Laura slaps her thigh. "My goodness. Your highness. I had no idea."

"Megan came second two years in a row. I told her it was all that giving birth that made her lose her edge. She always used to beat me, but not anymore."

"Can't wait to see that in action." Laura's face is as bright as I've ever seen it.

"You must have a go!"

"Who? A city slicker like me? I don't stand a chance." She boldly looks into my eyes, as though she's accepting a challenge.

I narrow my eyes. "You think you can beat me?"

Laura purses her lips and shakes her head. "Why would I think that? You're a ranch girl. You've probably been riding live bulls all your life."

"We don't ride bulls at the ranch, Laura."

She sits there grinning from ear to ear. I walked right into that one.

"Okay, hot shot, game on. Loser cooks the other one dinner."

"I'd best go shopping for a new cookbook then," Laura says.

I extend my hand, she looks at it for an instant, then shakes it. "I accept the challenge."

After we've finished our salads, she shows me the rosebushes she planted in the garden. While we overlook the greenery, I ask, "How are you doing?" I can hardly pretend that her confession didn't happen.

"I think it was good for me to say it out loud. Share it with someone." Laura examines one of the roses closely.

"Did you see someone… professional after it happened?"

"You mean a therapist?" Laura's still fascinated by the rose. "I did for a while, but for me, going for a run does so much more to exorcize my demons than saying the same things over and over again to someone I'm paying to listen."

"We have someone in Nelson, you know. I'm mentioning it just in case."

Laura looks up from her flower-examining. "Thanks. I actually saw them mentioned in *The Ledger*. But I'm done having my soul squeezed by a shrink. It's up to me now to learn to live with it. There's nothing anyone else can say or do now. It's all down to me. I know it's going to take time and that, perhaps, I will miss opportunities because of it." It feels as though Laura is squeezing *my* soul when she says this. "But I don't want you to miss out on anything because of this. This is not your battle, Tess. I appreciate you're here for me. I really do. But… don't wait for me to be ready. You'll let the best years of your life go by."

"Yes, boss," I say half-heartedly. "I'm already having such a good time now, though." I shoot Laura the most gentle smile I have in me.

"Wait until I kick your ass at the rodeo." With that, Laura turns and heads back to the patio.

15

LAURA

A few weeks later, at the rodeo, Tess kicks my ass, royally. I wouldn't have thought it possible with her long limbs and high center of gravity, but she held on to that bull as though her life depended on it, beating Megan in the process as well.

We spend the afternoon hanging around one of the local farms and, apart from Friday night home games, this seems to be the only other occasion the entire town comes out for. It's a fun day out and Tess and I stay to watch the professionals battle it out. There are seven contestants, all of whom have come to Nelson for this reason only. To our great delight, one of them is a woman, who takes on the men with gusto and bravado.

"It's been a while since we had a proper cowgirl in these parts," Tess says, casting her glance over the woman approvingly.

The bull rider is dressed in the right attire for today's business. Flannel shirt, black vest, low-slung jeans and a pair of cowboy boots. "If I'd run into this woman in Chicago, my gaydar would be pinging uncontrollably, but this is the countryside and you just can't tell."

"What are you insinuating, Laura?" Tess looks at me with an expression of faux-indignation on her face. "That us country girls all look like lesbians to you?"

I shake my head. "You're missing the point entirely." I elbow Tess in the arm so she looks over at the woman again. She's staring straight at us.

"She's handsome," I say when we've averted our gaze.

"Are you trying to get rid of me or something?" There's unexpected bite to Tess's tone. I guess there is a limit to our banter.

Megan and Scott come over and the woman disappears from our field of vision. I keep her in the back of my mind. Maybe we'll bump into her later.

"We're taking the kids home. They've had too much sugar," Scott says.

"No they haven't, hon. That's just how children behave in the middle of a Saturday afternoon when their friends are around," Megan counters.

"Are you going to the dance tonight?" Tess asks.

"No. Emma's got a cold coming on and I don't want to leave her with Mom and Dad for the night. She'll wake them up too often," Megan says.

Scott stands shaking his head in disbelief. "And now she'll wake us up ten times during the night."

"No darling," Megan says, "It's the weekend, which means you get up when the kids need one of us before dawn."

Scott rolls his eyes. "I don't know why I ever married a Douglas." He shoots me a quick wink.

"I'm an Ingersley now," Megan says. "Although it hasn't had much positive effect on me."

"I'm taking you home, woman," Scott says.

They say their goodbyes, gather their children and leave the rodeo fest.

"What do you say, Laura? Time for a disco nap before we get our dancing shoes on?" Tess asks.

I agree, while I remind myself that this dance is going to be something entirely different than what I'm used to from parties in Chicago.

"SHE'S HERE," I say to Tess, more to steer her attention away from the poor imitation of line dancing I'm doing than to actually let her know.

"Who?" Tess is, of course, a natural at line dancing. She's had a lifetime of practice.

"The cowgirl. She's at the bar. Knocking them back like a pro."

"What's with you and that woman? Are you trying to tell me something? If you're interested in her, be my guest, Laura." Tess keeps jutting her feet out rhythmically while she says this.

I grab her by the arm and coax her out of the line. "You know very well I'm not interested in her."

"It sure sounded like you were." Tess is actually sulking.

"What's the matter?" She has me worried now.

"You... you're trying to pawn me off to the first woman who walks into town and vaguely looks like she could be a lesbian. Like you've had enough of me."

"I put both hands on Tess's shoulders. "I'm sorry if I was being too pushy. I just wanted to make clear that you shouldn't hold back on my account."

"Oh, I know that. I know that very well." Tess seems a little angry.

"Do you want to step outside for a minute?" I drop my hands from her shoulders.

"No, Laura, I just want to dance. I just want to have a good time." Tess already has one foot back on the dance floor. She really does love her line dancing.

I back off and sit down at a table on the edge of the dance floor. I probably did push her too far. Like I was trying to live vicariously through her. I let my gaze roam over the dance floor, and over the simple but exquisite pleasure the dancers are experiencing. Automatically, I compare what I'm seeing to Chicago where the clubs are always trying to outdo each other when it comes to new technologies. But lasers and revolving podiums and ridiculously expensive DJs don't make happiness, I conclude. The simpler, the better. That's why I moved here.

I glance over at the bar, at the cowgirl. Even when she was riding the bull, and holding on for dear life, she kept a certain grace about her. Smile half-cocked, lips pursed in concentration, eyes on the prize. She came second and was very gracious about that as well.

While my glance skitters back from the cowgirl to Tess, I wonder if I would feel the slightest pang of jealousy if, hypothetically, the cowgirl managed to pick Tess up. I look at Tess strutting her stuff on the floor and, with a fierceness that surprises me, I conclude that I would be. I'm ashamed by my own selfishness. While it's silly to claim that I have no right to feel that way, that's how I see it. Because I can't give Tess what she wants. Can't even come close. Not even for a night. Not even for a minute.

I push any thoughts of Tracy to the back of my mind, sit back, and watch the dancers. Tess glances over in my direction again. The dancing must have lifted her spirits. She gives me a sort of wicked grin I haven't seen on her before and, instead of wondering about the consequences, or analyzing what she means by it and what I would say in my defense if it were to lead to us having a moment again, I just enjoy the view of my friend dancing and having a good time.

A few songs later, when the music has turned slow and Tess has turned down the invitation to dance from one of the cowboys, she sits next to me, and says, "You know what, Laura? I danced on it, and maybe you're right."

I quirk up my eyebrows, waiting for further explanation.

"If that cowgirl makes a move, I may not reject it. Emphasis on 'may', but it's a first step." To back up what she just said, Tess looks over at the woman and I witness how their gazes meet. I *am* jealous now. But that's my problem.

"Oh God, I think she's coming over." Tess looks at the table. "You have to help me, Laura. I'm so out of practice."

"No you're not," I say, "and I should know." This elicits a look from Tess I can't decipher.

"Howdy, ladies." The woman has reached our table. In one hand she holds a beer bottle, the other hand she clasps around her belt. "Aren't you two just the cutest couple I've seen."

"We're not a couple," Tess and I say simultaneously.

The woman gives a deep-throated laugh. "Okay. Got it." She has the same half-cocked smile on her face as this afternoon on the bull. "My name is Sherry and I came to this lovely little town to win the rodeo, but I didn't. So now I could do with some company. Do you mind if I join you?"

I let Tess do the talking. "Of course. Pull up a chair. I'm Tess, and this is Laura."

"I saw you strutting your stuff on the floor there, Tess. You've got moves, girl," Sherry says to Tess, then turns to me. "Not much of a dancer, are you? I'm the same."

"Laura's new in town. She's still learning," Tess says and shoots me a furtive glance. Is this my cue to leave? I did tell her I would be her wing woman if she needed me, but we have no practice at this and I don't know what the rules are. I guess I'll set the rules then.

"Moved here a few months ago." Up close, Sherry has a sort of rugged handsomeness that seldom works on a woman, but it does on her. She must get all the girls wherever she goes. She'd better treat Tess right. "Still building my business. Speaking of which, I just caught sight of Billy and I need to check in with him about something. Please excuse me."

I try to give Tess an encouraging smile. If she hadn't just said that she 'may' not reject Sherry's advances, I wouldn't have left her alone with the cowgirl. But it's sort of my duty to give her a push. If anything, it would be good for her to bask in the attention another woman bestows on her. For her life to revolve a little less around me for a night. I give her a quick tap on the shoulder and make my way to the bar. I don't see Billy anymore, nor do I have any business to discuss with him. I do run into Myriam and Isabella, who regale me with a tale of how their cat gave birth to the cutest litter of ginger kittens and ask me if I want to adopt one. I'm so absent-minded—I keep thinking about Tess and sneaking peeks at her—that I accept without even thinking about it.

16

TESS

I can't believe Laura left me alone with this woman so quickly. It's as if she's trying to prove something. Or trying to make a point at the very least. "Don't wait for me, Tess," she said. As if things like that just happen on command. As if I can just switch off my feelings because she's emotionally unavailable. And why did I say that about not automatically wanting to reject the cowgirl's advances? And how did I end up tête-à-tête with her so quickly? Maybe the universe is trying to tell *me* something—it must be in cahoots with Laura then.

"Are you from here? Ah, wait, don't tell me. I think you are," Sherry says.

She might be the nicest person on the planet, display the greatest amount of charm, and make me feel like one in a million, but I already know there's no way I'm going home with her tonight. Where would we go anyway? She doesn't live here. She's probably staying at the Nelson Inn and I wouldn't be caught dead there. It's not as if I could—if I wanted to, which I don't—take her home with me. Maybe I should ask Laura if we can use her house.

"You seem distracted," Sherry says. "Is it because your friend left so suddenly?"

She pins her light-blue gaze on me and, for a split second, she does make me feel like I'm the only person on the planet. What is it with this woman? Is she a witch or something? Does she have magical powers?

"No, I'm sorry." I can hardly pour out my heart to Sherry. "You have my undivided attention now." I pull my lips into a smile. "Do you go from town to town?" I might as well make the most of the situation and get to know Sherry's story. After all, it's not every day that you meet a female bull rider. And I'm nothing if not polite.

"I do." Sherry's 'I' is flatter than mine. "Travel all around Texas in my trailer. It's not a bad life. I get to meet inter-esting folks everywhere." Sherry has planted her elbows on the table and she leans in close. "Folks like yourself." Her smile goes all lop-sided. She's not just an excellent bull rider then.

"I'm guessing folks like myself are pretty rare in small-town Texas." I play along a little.

"You would think that, but I never have any trouble finding them." She sinks her teeth into her bottom lip.

"I bet." I sip from my beer; Sherry does the same. "So you go around the state leaving a trail of broken hearts?"

"Hardly." Sherry leans in a little closer. "There are plenty of women who are after exactly what I'm offering."

I mirror Sherry's position, our faces almost touching. "And what exactly are you offering?"

"A good time. A type of conversation you don't have every day. A different perspective. Things like that. Sometimes, when they really move me in here," Sherry slants back a bit and taps her chest, "I write them a poem."

"A poem? You're a woman of many talents." She's starting to intrigue me a little.

"I haven't done the research, but it could very well be that I'm the only cowgirl-poet out there."

Because my brain is trained this way, I have to ask. "How long are you in town for, Sherry?"

"Wanting to keep me already." Her eyes glitter with promise. "I usually stick around a week or so. Sometimes longer. No use traveling all this way to just up and leave all the time."

"I run the local gazette and I would love to interview you for it. The cowgirl-poet is an excellent angle. We could even publish one of your poems."

"How about the one I write for you, Tess?"

I have to chuckle. She's good. And that smooth voice of hers is winning me over. "We'll see about that. Do you have a phone number where I can reach you after the weekend?"

"If it were up to me, you wouldn't need a phone, but sure." She picks a pen out of the breast pocket of her shirt. "Give me your hand."

I look at the pen, then at my hand, trying to put the pieces together. "Really?"

"U-hum." Sherry gives a slow nod.

I hold out my hand, palm up, and allow her to scribble her number on it. "It'll be gone as soon as I wash my hands."

Sherry cocks her head. "I believe in what's meant to be, Tess. If you're meant to call me, you will have that number when you need it. Either way, this is a small town. You'll see me around."

I've been so wrapped up in Sherry's words that I didn't notice Laura heading toward our table. She has a stressed look on her face.

"Sorry to disturb." Laura runs a nervous hand through her hair. "I just got a call from Windsor Oaks. Aunt Milly has taken a turn for the worse. They've taken her to the hospital in, uh, Forreston. I have to go." She stands there looking so forlorn and alone.

"I'll go with you," I say instinctively. "I'll show you the way."

Sherry leans back in her chair, regarding the scene.

"Tess, there's no need. Just stay here. I'll call you tomorrow." Laura starts to turn already.

"Go," Sherry mouths.

"Laura, wait. I'm coming." I grab my purse and jacket and pace after her, put an arm on her shoulder. "What did they say?"

"Nothing much. Just to hurry."

And hurry we do.

LAURA

The drive over is tense, the silence only broken up by Tess giving me directions. At the hospital, they make us wait.

"Thank you for coming with me," I say. "I'm so glad I don't have to be here alone."

"Don't mention it," Tess says. "Shall I get us some tea? It might be a long night."

"I'll go with you." We walk to a machine at the end of the corridor. "She hasn't been doing very well. It's as though I've been watching her slip away more and more." Though I've been expecting this moment, it still feels like someone is clenching an ice-cold fist around my heart.

"Whatever happens, Laura, you've been there for her. You were a daily presence in her life. That counts for a lot."

We walk back to the cluster of chairs in the waiting room and sit down. "I know what it feels like to be alone. That's why I came to Nelson, but, you know, it was a bit of a last ditch effort. Before I arrived here, she'd probably been feeling alone for quite some time already."

Tess puts her hand on my knee. "You're looking at it the wrong way. First of all, she lived in Nelson, and before she broke her hip, she was still very mobile and got to see enough people during the day. Second, you were hardly in a state to think of anyone but yourself." Her hand remains on my knee.

"I didn't get to ask her the million dollar question, though." I wanted to. Every day, I wanted to. But, somehow, I couldn't bring myself to let their names flow from my lips.

"What's that?"

"Whether, when the time came, she wanted her brother and his wife invited to the memorial." That cold fist is there again, clenching for a different reason now.

"Your parents?" Tess's hand squeezes.

"Richard and Phyllis Baker. The people who raised me but stopped being my parents long ago."

"Did they get along?" Tess asks.

"Heavens no. My father never approved of Uncle George. Nowhere near Christian enough."

"You might still get a chance to ask her."

"I hope so." Tess removes her hand and stares at her palm while a sliver of a smile appears on her face.

"What's that." I see something on her hand.

She shows it to me. "Sherry gave me her number. I may interview her for *The Ledger*."

I can't believe I was jealous earlier. I just want Tess to be happy now. "Sorry for interrupting your, huh, whatever it was."

"I would never have gone back with her. I told you I'm not one for one-night stands." Tess's voice goes all hushed, as though this is not something to discuss in a hospital waiting room. "But it was nice to... I don't know... do some heavy flirting. She's a poet."

"A poet?" I don't get the chance to ask more, because a doctor is coming our way.

"Are you the relatives of Millicent Johnson?"

"Yes." I rise and wipe my sweaty palms on my jeans.

"She's in intensive care. She took a nasty fall. Hit her head.

She's stable for now. You can see her, but she's not conscious. Taking into account her advanced age and overall health I think you should prepare for the worst." The doctor is young, but he delivers his words in a gentle but confident manner, his gaze unwavering.

I nod my understanding, though the words don't really get through just yet.

"Family only." The doctor walks off.

I look at Tess, wishing she could go in with me.

"Laura, come here." She opens her arms.

Without thinking, I step into her embrace, choking away a tear.

"I'll be right here waiting," Tess whispers in my ear. "Take all the time you need."

AUNT MILLY LOOKS as frail as I've ever seen her. She's connected to a monitor that beeps steadily. An oxygen mask is on her face. I can still see some dried blood in her hair, although the nurses have tried to clean it off. And the sight of her floors me. My stomach crumples, my knees go a little weak, and I need to steady myself against the wall. She's the only family I have left. The only person with Baker blood running through her veins that I know. She and Uncle George never had children. My mom has three sisters, but I never met any of them. I probably have a bunch of cousins out there but, if I do, I've never heard of them.

"My family has never been a good influence on me," my mom told me when I was little. "I was better off without them." Then I became better off without my family too—except for Aunt Milly.

What I've always wondered though, is why devout Christians like my parents, who vocally disapproved of contraception, never had more children. I never asked. I shake off the thought and look at my aunt. It's as though I can sense that, no matter if she recovers from this head injury, these are her last days on this earth.

I look at her and wonder what she would want. "I forgive him," she once told me. "I forgive my brother for being a bigoted ass, which makes me, a heathen as he would call me, a much better person than him. How's that for irony?"

Does that mean she would want him to pay her his last respects? Then I ask myself the only question that will solve this issue for me. Would I want my parents to come to my last send-off? I find it impossible to give a quick yes or no, though I've always tried to consider them as no longer existing in the same world as me. Why is it so hard to shake them off completely?

I postpone making my decision. Aunt Milly is still alive and, as long as she is, I'll be by her side.

18

TESS

Laura is spending all her time at the hospital. She takes her laptop to Aunt Milly's room and works from there. "Just so I'm there when she wakes up."

I wait until Wednesday to call Sherry. After Laura went into her aunt's room at the hospital, I quickly copied her phone number on a piece of paper, before it had the chance to fade away.

When I meet her for coffee at Mary's, we've barely sat down before she asks, "How's Laura's aunt doing?" Sherry's kindness already came through on Saturday night when she was flirting with me. It shone through her bluster and bravado so easily, which is probably why I enjoyed her flirting with me so much.

"It's not looking good. She has woken up a few times, but the prognosis is not hopeful."

"I'm so sorry to hear that." Sherry couldn't sound more sincere. That must be how she does what she does, conquering hearts—or other body parts—across Texas. She's an expert at making people feel special and that's hard to resist.

"Laura is pretty cut up about it."

103

"Understandably." Sherry clears her throat. "So you and Laura, huh?"

Of course I know what she's getting at, but, for my own sanity, I need to play dumb. "What about me and Laura?" I can't even make my voice sound genuine.

"It's very clear to me that you love her. I barely know you, yet I can't ignore it. I don't want to be stepping on anyone's toes here." She rests her chin on her palms, strokes her cheeks with her fingers.

"I know what it looks like. But it's very complicated and there's a very good reason why Laura and I aren't together." Not an hour goes by that I don't think about that reason.

"U-hum." Sherry does that low, slightly cynical hum I've heard her utter quite a few times. "There always is."

I inhale sharply. "But you're right. I have feelings for her." Though it's a relief to be able to just blurt it out to someone, Sherry is perhaps not the best choice of person to confide in. I'd better bring us back to the order of the day. "So, about our interview."

She pulls her lips into a lopsided smile. "I don't care to be interviewed, Tess. I'm glad you called me, but I'd rather keep myself under the radar, so to speak."

"But… you said…"

Sherry reaches her hand across the table and touches my forearm with her fingers gently. "I think I can safely presume we both know why we're here." She looks me straight in the eyes, her stare bold and unblinking.

A fierce blush creeps all the way up from my neck to my cheeks. If I say something now, it will surely come out as an inadequate stammer. I give a slow nod while I suck on my bottom lip. I return Sherry's stare, though mine doesn't feel half as bold as hers.

I called her. Under the pretense of interviewing her for *The Ledger*, yes, but, deep down, I knew what it would really be

FAR FROM THE WORLD WE KNOW

about—like Sherry just said. I took the necessary steps to see her again. I wanted to see her again, because I liked how she made me feel. As little as I know about her, I know enough to see she's good at heart. So, the only question that remains now is: do I want her?

"How about dinner tonight?" Sherry says, her fingers still on my skin. "No strings attached." She's still gazing into my eyes. To me, it seems she wants to seal the deal here and now.

Then the door of the café opens, I look up briefly, and see that it's Laura, and in that instant I know for certain that, no matter how nice Sherry's fingers on my arm make me feel, how wanted and craved for, I will never go anywhere with her. Because the woman I want just walked in the door and our eyes met only for the briefest of moments, and still I knew.

Sherry turns to see whose presence in the café has thrown me, then looks at me again, her smile a little sad. "I'm going to leave you to it, Tess." She starts to get up.

"I'll call you," I mutter.

Sherry takes a step in my direction, puts a hand on my shoulder, and says, "There's no need." She leans in and kisses me slowly, gently on the cheek. "See ya, Tess." She gives a quick two-fingered wave to Laura and leaves the café.

I lean back in my chair and give a few minutes of thought to how thrilling it felt to be truly wanted by someone else for a few minutes. I watch Laura as she orders a tea to go. In the two short encounters I had with Sherry, she made me feel more desirable than Laura has in the entire time I've known her. I don't hold it against her, because how could I possibly do that? Nevertheless, it stings. It hurts to want someone who can't reciprocate. Who explicitly told me not to wait for her.

"Hey." While Mary brews her tea, Laura comes over. "I hope I didn't interrupt anything."

"Turns out I'm not the kind of gal who goes off to make sweet sweet love to the cowgirl passing through town." Truth is, I couldn't even imagine it. As charming as Sherry is, every time I tried to picture us together, Laura's face emerged. Maybe I will have to start keeping my distance, but what kind of friend would that make me? It's as though, because of what Laura told me about herself, I'm now tethered to her because I want to be there for her as a friend, but I'm always kept at a safe distance as well. I don't even have the option of walking away to preserve my own sanity, to safeguard *my* own heart.

"Sorry," Laura says. She just stands there and in her demeanor—hesitant, wavering—she's the opposite of the woman who just sat across from me, and I suddenly find it infuriating.

"Why are you sorry?"

"I don't know."

"Can we talk for a second." I motion for her to sit.

"Sure." She sits across from me, like she has done so many times before, but, this time, it feels different.

"How's Aunt Milly?" I can't just barge into what I'm about to tell her, though the rage I felt initially, and that was spurring me on to have this conversation with her, is quickly dissipating now that I'm looking into those blue eyes again.

"The same." She's not in a very communicative mood then.

And I can't bring myself to say it. The line I was going to feed her: *my head knows I need some distance, but my heart wants other things.*

Deserting Laura now would make me feel much worse than all the useless pining for her does.

"What did you want to talk about?" Laura asks when I don't say anything.

"Have you, er, made a decision yet," I say instead of what I wanted to say. While I do, I think of what I said to Laura the night she told me about her deceased wife. *I refuse to play the martyr because of how I feel about you.* I sure as hell feel like one now. "About your parents?"

"I've sat with the phone in my hands a couple of times. I had to find their number first, so I went online and looked at both their faces on the church's website. Such a nice, smiling couple they make. Dashing really. You'd never guess they once told their daughter to fuck off." Laura scratches her neck. "I—I sent them an invitation when Tracy and I got married. To the church, because I don't even know if they still live at the same address. The silence afterward was deafening. Not a word from them."

"I'm so sorry." Instinctively, I reach for Laura's hand over the table—as though my touch can make it better.

"No need to feel sorry for me. Besides, that has nothing to do with Aunt Milly, who did attend the wedding, by the way. Came all the way from Texas. This was before she broke her hip." Laura doesn't shrug my hand off her. "I figure that even if I let them know about Aunt Milly's condition, they probably won't show up anyway. That they will just remain silent. Why would they forgive her for marrying someone as inappropriate as Uncle George now? My father will probably try to get her into heaven on her deathbed or something." Laura's voice is growing high-pitched.

"Do you still want that to go?" Mary comes over with Laura's tea.

"Oh, no, I'll just have it here. Thanks, Mary."

"You give Milly my love, okay?" Mary says. "Tell her to pull through."

We watch Mary shuffle off. Her appearance has diminished the anger in Laura's eyes a little.

"Are you religious?" I ask. The arrival of Laura's tea has my hand lying limply—and stupidly—next to her arm.

"Not in the tiniest bit." Laura straightens her spine. "I'll save you the speech that usually goes with that statement. Though I know my parents are fundamentalists, and the thought of a higher power means a lot to many people, and there's a big difference between the two." Her shoulders sag again. "But in my world, religion has done so much more damage than good." She regards me intently. "How about you?"

"We're surely taking this a step further," I joke, because I think the conversation needs it. "We've moved on to discussing God."

"You don't have to answer." Laura removes the lid from her cup and starts blowing on it.

"No, it's fine. I really don't mind." My joke was clearly lost on Laura. "You've met my parents. You know they're pretty casual—"

I'm interrupted by the loud chime of a phone—Laura's.

She nearly jumps out of her chair. "I turned up the volume," she says apologetically. "Sorry, I need to take this. It's the hospital." Her movements are tense, her lips drawn into a thin line.

"Hello," she says, as she listens to the person on the other end of the line. Then her face goes blank.

19

LAURA

Tess must know that, without her by my side, I'd be crumbling right now. I wouldn't be able to do what I'm about to do. She's so strong, so unwavering in her support of me, despite me not being able to give her what she wants, that sometimes, usually late at night, I can almost see it. I can see us together. Because to me, she's a rock. She's always there with a joke to cheer me up, and a facial expression full of understanding when I need it.

"Do you want me to call them?" she offers now. "I can pretend to be someone working at the hospital informing Aunt Milly's next of kin."

The thing about Tess is that, when she says things like that, she's dead serious about them. "I need to do this myself," I say.

"Shall I go into the other room?" Sometimes, when she looks at me like this, her face all earnest and her eyes all kindness, I actually feel a twinge of desire to kiss her run through me.

"No, I want you here with me."

Tess nods solemnly. "I'm here." And that little phrase couldn't sum up Tess more. She's always here for me. Always.

"Okay. Here we go." I dial the number I found on the website. I'm guessing it won't be a direct line to the anointed Pastor Richard, but someone will be able to put me through.

"Hello, First Light Church. How may I help you?"

My heart pounds in my throat. "This is Laura Baker, the pastor's daughter. Can I speak with him?"

"I'm very sorry, Laura. Pastor Richard is holding a sermon right now. Can I help?"

"What about Phyllis? His wife?" I wouldn't be caught dead calling that woman my mother to a stranger. "Can I speak with her? It's a family emergency."

An exasperated sigh at the other end of the line. "Hold on, Laura." The voice still sounds overly friendly and cheerful, though. "I may be able to whisk her out. Please hold." I hear a dull click, then a hymn sounds through the speaker. Because some things in life you just never forget, I instantly recognize it as "Abide With Me". I must have sung along to it a million times when I was a child. I still know the words by heart.

"I'm on hold," I whisper to Tess. "Listen to this. The sound-track to my youth." I hold the phone to her ear. Meanwhile, my heart flings itself against my ribcage with increasing fervor. I haven't heard my mother's voice in more than a decade. What will it do to me now? They know nothing about my life, about what I've been through. If they did, they'd probably end up praying for me. Maybe they've prayed for my corrupted soul daily over the years.

"Hello?" A voice crackles over the phone. It's not the same voice as before. It's a voice I've tried to forget but never could. It's the voice of Phyllis Baker. The voice of my mother.

"It's Laura." Automatically, a hardness creeps into my tone. "Aunt Milly passed away this morning. I thought you should know."

"Oh," my mother says. "I'm very sorry to hear that."

I don't say anything, unsure if it's just plain reluctance on my part, or pure disdain flaring up—disdain for how she's not falling apart right now, for how she sounds so emotionless. Does she really not care that it's me she's speaking to?

"The memorial service will be next weekend, here in Nelson. I'll send an invitation." I'm ready to hang up. I've done my duty. Now that Aunt Milly's gone, I have no family left.

"I'm not sure we'll be able to make it. Your father has a lot of obligations during the weekend."

"Fine." The phone is starting to shake against my ear. Without expressing a goodbye, I hang up. I stare at the phone for long seconds, unable to process the coldness I encountered on the other end of the line. Or was my mother's heart pounding in her chest as well? Were her palms so sweaty the phone threatened to slip out of her hands? Does she ever think about the child she gave birth to forty-one years ago?

"What did she say?" Tess rises from her seat and stands next to me. I know she's cautious about hugging me—and I know how much that goes against her very nature.

"Nothing, really." I find her gaze briefly, then open my arms and throw them around her. Because I need human contact to get past this moment. I need someone's arms around me.

When Tess's hands meet behind my back, and I feel her warmth, and, perhaps, also her affection for me, the tension that had lodged itself inside my gut releases and, to my great dismay, I crack. I let go and cry on Tess's shoulder. I cry for the loss of Aunt Milly. I cry for the child I was when my parents didn't hate me yet. I cry for the life I took, and how it's, slowly, sapping the life right out of me as well. I cry for the bruises that healed and the ones that didn't.

"Hey." Tess's hand is on the back of my head now. "Let it all out, sweetie. Just let it all out."

What would I have done if Tess wasn't here to comfort me? If I hadn't met her, if she didn't know. If I hadn't had anyone to share this with? The thought is so acute, it makes me draw in a deep breath and lift my head from her shoulder, find her eyes.

"I don't know what I'd do without you." As the words leave my lips, I realize how utterly weak that sounds. How unlike the woman I wanted to become after Tracy. Free of codependence. Of that gnawing feeling that without the other person, I might as well cease to exist. Free of the shackles that tethered me to Tracy for way too long, through the physical pain—although, when it came down to it, the emotional damage Tracy inflicted was a million times worse. Bruises heal, but self-confidence is much harder to restore.

"I'm here, so no need to think about that." I detect a mist of tears in Tess's eyes as well.

And then, perhaps because I want to forget, or because I don't want to be this post-Tracy person anymore, or because I remember those distinct pangs of jealousy when Sherry was making moves on Tess, I tilt my head and press my lips to Tess's.

She doesn't kiss me back. Her lips remain stiff and don't curve the way I want them to, don't melt into mine the way I had anticipated.

Mortified, I pull back. "I, er, I thought you wanted this?"

"Oh, Laura." Tess's hands find mine and she squeezes my fingers tightly between hers. "I do. You know I do, but not now. You're reeling with emotion. It's not the right time."

"I just… want to forget. Everything," I stammer.

"I know." She's not afraid to look me straight in the eyes while I, my nerves frayed and my confidence shot to pieces, have trouble holding her gaze. "But I'm not someone you can use to just forget about things, Laura. If and when we do this, I want it to come from a real place. From the opposite of grief and pain."

I understand. Of course, I understand. But it still feels like a rejection at the worst possible time. I give her a reluctant nod.

"Why don't we sit down for a bit. Let's talk. Would that be okay?"

I nod again.

"Gosh, I do wish I could pour you a nice strong glass of bourbon right now," Tess says.

"If I had any in the house, I wouldn't object."

"Aunt Milly didn't keep a secret stash?" There's a hint of hope in her voice. I'm guessing Tess could do with a drink too.

"Oh, she did, but I threw it all out when I moved in." It was the very first thing I did when I arrived. Like a ritual, I poured all the remaining booze down the drain, its smell making me sick to the stomach. As though I held alcohol solely responsible for what I did to Tracy and getting rid of it was like a cleansing of sorts, a way to get the house ready for my presence. For a chance to heal.

Tess smiles one of her warmest smiles. "Come on. We don't need booze." She puts an arm around me and coaxes me toward the sofa, where she sits next to me with the side of her thigh glued to mine. And I realize that it's all I need, a little bit of Tess's warmth, and a sign that what she just said to me wasn't a rejection, but a display of having my best interests at heart.

"You've been through a lot, Laura. It's okay to crumble a little, or a lot. As much as you like." We don't look at each other, just stare at the opposite wall, at a painting of a Texas landscape that I wanted to keep.

"I don't know what I was expecting from that call." It's easier to talk with no one looking at me directly. "Maybe a small part of me wanted her to say... something. I wasn't looking for an apology. Just, maybe a sign that she was glad to hear my voice, that I had established contact."

"Laura, honestly, from what you've told me about your family, you're better off without them. And I know placing that call was very hard for you to do, and you should be glad you did it and it's over, so you don't need to feel guilty about not notifying them. But you have done absolutely nothing wrong."

"That's what Tracy used to say." It comes out as a strangled whisper. "Until she started accusing me of doing *everything* wrong." I'm digging deep now, saying things I've only ever thought, never said out loud. "Sometimes I wonder whether I fell for her because I craved the sort of love she was asking for. Complete and total surrender. Devotion, really. The kind of love my parents gave to the church, but not to me. Not after I came out. And when Tracy"—I need to catch my breath—"punished me for not abiding by one of her crazy, made-up on-the-fly rules, deep down, I believed I deserved it."

Tess's hand shuffles up my thigh. She clamps her fingers in a tight grip around mine. She doesn't speak immediately. Maybe she doesn't have anything to say. Maybe she's waiting for me to continue. When I don't, she says with a shaky voice, "Laura, you've just been so unlucky. Nobody deserves to be treated like that by their parents, nor their partner. You do know you're not to blame for any of this?"

Tears prick in my eyes. I hold on to Tess's hand for dear life. "I know I'm not responsible for how my parents see me… like an abomination—my father's exact term for it, by the way. I was born to them, but I didn't choose them as my family. I did choose Tracy, though. I married her. I took her last name. For more than a year, I was Laura Hunt. And I let her…" A choke in my voice so big, the words can't get past anymore.

Tess turns to me now and lifts my hand in the process, cradles it in both her own. "You were the victim of abuse. You did absolutely nothing wrong."

With my free hand, I wipe away the tears that have gathered on my cheeks. "I stayed, though. After she first… came for me, I didn't walk away. I didn't have the strength, or the self-respect, or wherewithal to leave her. And God knows how long I would have stayed if I hadn't—if she hadn't died."

"Relationships are much more complex than just up-and-leaving when one party hurts the other." Tess shakes her head. "You are not to blame."

"I know. I know that now." Most of the time I do know. "But today, after hearing my mother's voice, and the complete lack of any display of affection in it, it just got to me, I guess. As much as I don't want it to, and I don't want them to have any effect over me, it still gets to me. Even though I know that there's nothing I could have done to change things."

"Can I make a suggestion?" Tess tilts her head a little. "Come to dinner at my house tonight. Spend some time with the Douglas clan. Have a real family dinner for once. You're not alone, Laura." She gives my hand a squeeze. "Only if you're up to it, of course."

I nod, hesitantly at first, but then with more gusto. Because I don't feel like spending the evening in Aunt Milly's house, which feels somehow more empty and big now that she's gone. I also refuse to feel sorry for myself for one minute longer.

"Great." Tess draws her lips into a warm smile.

"I'm sorry about before, about kissing you. I shouldn't have—"

"It's okay." My hand is still trapped in hers.

"No. I wasn't taking your feelings into account. I was unfair."

"Laura, listen to me. Put yourself first. There's nothing wrong with that. But if it makes you feel any better, apology accepted."

20

TESS

A few days later, after I minded the kids for a while so Megan could attend a Zumba class while Scott was at a staff meeting, I tell my sister about the kiss.

"She kissed you?" Megan asks. "The woman you've had a massive crush on for the past two months kissed you, and you didn't kiss her back?" She shakes her head in disbelief. "What is wrong with you, Tessie?"

"It couldn't have been a worse time." When I close my eyes, I can still feel Laura's lips on mine. "Her aunt had just died. She'd just been on the phone with her heartless mother. It wouldn't have been for the right reasons."

"You know, Tessie, sometimes I think celibacy is a conscious choice for you. First the cowgirl, now this."

"Let me assure you that it's not." That hug Laura gave me a few days ago still lingers, still makes me want everything I can't have. "But I want it to be right. Is that so crazy?"

"No, I guess not, but this is life. And more often than not, it's messy and doesn't go according to plan. Things just happen." Megan eyes me with that look she gets when she's playing devil's advocate. When we were younger, we broke out into the occasional sibling fight, but it's rare that we argue. Perhaps this type of back and forth is our way of doing so.

"The cowgirl was attractive in a very... primal way. She had this air about her, this supreme confidence that was magnetic, and if it hadn't been for Laura, I'd probably be in her trailer right now. I don't know. But that's the thing. Ever since Laura arrived, I just..." My eloquence escapes me for a second.

"You've pinned all your hopes and dreams on her." Another one of my sister's habits: finishing my sentences with words I would never say.

"No, I haven't." It's more defiance than anything else that makes me tell this lie—to my sister *and* to myself.

"Why are you lying?" Megan isn't one to let me get away with this.

I raise my arms in exasperation. "I don't know, Megs. I like her. When I spend time with her, I can sense... the possibilities."

"Yes, but she's obviously stringing you along. Why?" Megan had better be careful. She's about to cross a line we seldom cross.

"She's doing no such thing." I wish I could tell my sister, explain it to her properly, but I gave Laura my word. "She's had a really tough life, okay? A life you and I can't even begin to imagine. She's been hurt over and over again. She's still healing."

"So you feel sorry for her?"

"No. I mean, yes, I do. Of course, I do. But feeling sorry for Laura isn't going to help her. We're friends. For now. And yes, I hope that will change at some point, but that's not up to me. Is that okay with you, Megan?" I hardly ever call my sister by her full name. Doing so must alert her to the fact that she's seriously annoying me.

"I just don't want you to get hurt."

"What's the worst that can happen?"

"So many things could happen. But you don't see them as a possibility because your eyes are glazed over with lust for a woman who doesn't want to be with you." Megan's face has gone all serious. "She could lean on you for a few more months, get tired of Nelson, and just leave. There's nothing tying her to the place now that her aunt is gone."

"Nu-uh. No way."

"Look, Tessie, what I'm trying to say is that—and you should take this as a compliment—any woman would be lucky to have you bestow your attentions upon her. You're a ray of light. It's your nature. Of course someone who has been hurt, like you say Laura has been, is going to try to cling to that. Just, you know, make sure *you* get something out of it as well."

"Dear Megs, I sort of love you for saying that, but you have no idea what you're talking about."

Megan holds up her hands. "Perhaps, but I don't want my sister to get hurt. That's all."

"I appreciate your concern, but I'm a big girl. And Laura's not out to hurt me. She's a good person... with issues."

"One last question, and then I'll leave you be," Megan says. "She seems like a nice enough woman, and she's got it going on in the looks department, but what's so special about her anyway?"

"Really?" For the first time in a very long time, Megan has offended me greatly. "You're really asking me that?"

"Too much?" Regret crosses Megan's face. "I'm sorry."

"It's fine, I'll answer." I wouldn't give Megan the satisfaction of not coming up with a great response to her inappropriate question. "We definitely have a vibe. She makes me laugh, and makes me feel good about myself, and makes me want to do nice things for her, and be there for her. And when she kissed me, it was the hardest thing ever to not just kiss her back, but I respect her too much to have just reciprocated. And yes, I'm smitten. I will gladly admit to that. Because why the hell

119

wouldn't I be? Laura is a beautiful, sensitive, sweet, very talented woman."

"Okay. Okay." Megan breaks out into a grin. "I get it. You've made your case. You have my blessing to pine for her a little while longer. But if she hurts you, she'll have me to deal with."

"Not that I need your blessing for anything just because we shared a womb, but thanks for looking out for me."

"That's what family is for."

"And babysitting," I add.

"That goes without saying." Megan winks at me and, again, I think of Laura, who, in a few days' time, will be burying the one remaining family member she cared for.

21

LAURA

Rachel has come down from Chicago for Aunt Milly's funeral. Apart from her, at the service at the cemetery, the only people I know better than as a mere acquaintance or a familiar face from around town, are Tess, her family, Mary from the café, Myriam and Isabella, and a few locals I've been doing some work for. Still, the turn-out for Aunt Milly's send-off is numerous and, though it hardly still matters now, I think that would have pleased her.

When I made arrangements for the service, the minister asked if I wanted to say a few words, but I declined the offer. I'd rather say goodbye in silence. The way I did when Tracy died. Her funeral was one of the most harrowing times of my life. People who didn't know what had happened saw me as the grieving widow, while her family and friends saw me as her killer. I counted myself in the second group.

Burying Aunt Milly today, makes me think about death again, and about how fragile life is. One wrong step, and it can be over and done with. When you've seen the life drain out of someone's eyes right in front of you, and when you've caused that to happen, and have come face-to-face with how breakable the human body can be, it changes everything. At least Aunt Milly lived a full, long life. No matter what Tracy did to me, I took that away from her. I robbed her of a future. I robbed her parents of a child.

I should be listening to what the minister is saying, but I've become so averse to words spoken by clerical folks, I don't really care what he has to say. It's the same old stuff anyway. God this, Jesus that. What did God do with Tracy when she came knocking on heaven's door? Did he let her in? Forgive her for her earthly sins and take her into his divine embrace? My father said this to me after I came out to him. If you repent, and don't give in to your unnatural urges, God will embrace you. But it was not God's embrace I was after. It was his.

I look to my left. Rachel has slotted her arm through mine, and she has a solemn expression on her face. I try to get her attention by looking at her a fraction too long. I need to let someone know how much this funeral is messing with my head. How much it's bringing everything that's not right in my life together in my mind. But Rachel keeps staring at the coffin, her face stoic and serene. I try Tess on my right. Sweet Tess, who, after my little breakdown, took me home to share a meal with her family, and showed me what family is really about.

I don't know if she'd somehow prompted him, but Earl told the story of when Tess came out of the closet and his and his wife's reaction to that.

"We always knew. We were basically just waiting for Tessie to tell us. We didn't want to force that out of her." That was it. No drama. No guilt. No penance required to merit the embrace of God.

This makes me think of that short but awkward phone call with my mother again. And how glad I am that my father was too busy to attend his only sister's funeral. Pastor Baker only has time to lead a service for people he's not related to by blood.

How much longer is this going to take? I need to make it through this. Then through the funeral reception at the house which, now, is legally mine. I own a house in Nelson, Texas. I've never owned any property before. I take a deep breath and focus on the minister. Does he have children? What would he say to them if one of them came out as gay? Would he crush them in that most vulnerable time of their life? Or offer them God's embrace through his?

In the distance, I see a car approach. A black town car of the sort you seldom see in Nelson. It looks like a vehicle a mobster would drive. It inches closer and stops where the road ends, parking behind the funeral home's hearse. *Classy*, I think, though I am intrigued as to who would do such a thing. Who would drive up here in the middle of a service and park in the middle of the street?

When the car doors open, even before I catch a glimpse of who's about to come out, I know. It's them. It can only be them. A moment later my suspicion is confirmed. With their heads held high, as though they didn't just arrive at a funeral in the most disrespectful manner—and half an hour late—Richard and Phyllis Baker approach.

"Who's that?" Tess whispers in my ear. "Do you know them?"

"I wish I didn't, but I do." I take another deep breath. "They're my parents."

A buzz of whisperings passes through the crowd as the Bakers approach. They stop just outside the circle of people. Inadvertently, I find my father's gaze. Does he even recognize me? He gives me a slow nod, his features unreadable. I guess he does. I give him a hard stare back, then look away.

"Are you all right?" Tess whispers in my ear.

I don't even know what to say to that.

From my left, Rachel inquires, "Are they who I think they are?" Already, indignation is the main note in her voice.

I nod, hoping to answer both their questions at once.

The priest is unperturbed by the goings-on, and finishes the sermon. When everybody says 'Amen' I can hear my father's voice the loudest.

———

After the service ends, I don't know what to do. So I just stand there a while longer, accepting people's condolences with a meek smile on my face. But I can't keep my eyes off *them*. Their presence hangs over me like the darkest cloud. Oh, how I regret making that call now.

"You don't have to talk to them," Rachel says. "You don't owe them a goddamn thing."

"Would you like me to go over?" Tess points at them with her thumb, as though they're a mere nuisance to be dealt with. They are. "I can talk to them."

"It's fine. Just give me a minute."

"Do you want me to pretend I'm your girlfriend?" Rachel asks.

This elicits a nervous chuckle from Tess.

I extract myself from our circle of three and head over though, as I do, I fear my legs may give way. When I reach them, my father, typically, has already found an opportunity to talk to the minister, so I don't say anything. I wait until he catches a glimpse of me.

"Laura." He opens his arms wide, as if he wants to give me a hug. "Laura, my daughter." To my relief, he doesn't go for a fully-fledged hug, he just touches his palms to my shoulders lightly. But it's still too much.

"Please, don't touch me." At least my voice is still working.

"Laura," my mother, the woman who couldn't bring herself to say anything of importance to me on the phone when I called her, says, "we came." She says it as though they made the biggest sacrifice, flying out here and renting that ludicrous car.

"You're a bit late."

"Through no fault of our own. Our flight was delayed," my mother says.

I feel like walking away from her there and then without saying another word. Why would I waste any of my time talking to someone who can't even say sorry for arriving late at a funeral?

"We're very sorry about that, Laura," my father says. "Sadly, Millicent and I hadn't been on very good terms for a while, but I do know she was always a stickler for punctuality. We should have booked an earlier flight."

"Is there a reception?" my mother asks. Her face is turned toward me but she doesn't look straight at me. Her glance shoots right past.

If I had known they'd be coming, I would not have done it at the house. "Yes."

"We only have a few hours. We need to catch a flight out of Houston tonight," my father says.

"I'm sure this is all very inconvenient for you," I say.

That shuts them both up for a minute.

"Look, Laura," my father starts to say. "We would love to get a chance to—"

"Hey," someone shouts from the side of the road, "can someone move this black sedan? It's blocking everyone's way."

"Oh, heavens. I told you, Richard," my mother says.

"I have to go." I start turning away from them. "People will start arriving at the house soon. Just follow the crowd."

I walk back to where Tess and Rachel are standing. Tess's family has joined them.

"Are those your folks?" Earl asks.

"Afraid so." For some reason, I can't look him in the eyes

when I say this. I'm ashamed of them. Is that how they feel about me?

"Are they coming to yours?" Tess asks, her voice full of concern.

"Yep."

"We'll meet you all there, okay?" Tess addresses her family.

When it's just her, me, and Rachel left, she asks, "Are you sure you're all right?"

I just shrug because, inside, I feel as dead as Aunt Milly's body in the coffin we just watched being lowered into the ground.

TESS

At the house, Rachel and I try to hover around Laura as much as possible, but it's inevitable that she gets drawn into conversations with friends of Milly, the manager of the nursing home and, at one point, what appears to be a long talk with Myriam and Isabella.

I have my own social courtesies to adhere to as I know most of the people present in Laura's house much better than she does. But, from the corner of my eye, I watch her and conclude that, even though she doesn't perceive herself that way, she's one of the strongest people I've ever met. To go through today with the dignity that she has takes courage and a whole load of strength of character.

No thanks to them, I think, as I glance over at Laura's parents who awkwardly sit on a couple of chairs. Why did they even come here?

"Refill?" Rachel asks, holding up a bottle of red wine.

"Gladly." I offer her my empty glass. I'm so happy she's here, staying with Laura through this ordeal. I watch her make the rounds, most people gratefully accepting her offer to top up their drinks.

"Booze and funerals go hand in hand," she says, after she's emptied the bottle.

"Not for everyone." Laura hasn't touched a drop.

"True enough." Rachel nods. "Though Lord knows she could use a drink."

"She sure could." Our gazes meet and we exchange a knowing look. I remember what Laura said to me when she told me about Tracy, that Rachel was the only person who knew what went on between Tracy and her. "She told me," I say in a low voice. "I know what happened with Tracy."

Rachel is silent for an instant, as though considering her words. "It was a tragedy. And I don't just mean her death. I mean the whole thing, the entire marriage." Rachel shakes her head. "If it had been up to me, Tracy's family would have found out exactly what kind of person their daughter was, but Laura wouldn't have any of that. 'What does it matter now?' she asked. I thought it mattered a great deal, but I also understood that she was ashamed. With what she's been through," she lets some air escape from between her teeth, "I have no fucking clue how she picked herself up. Moving here has helped. I can see that. She has more confidence about her. When I arrived here, she even gave me a real, genuine smile. One from the heart. One that showed that moving here has been the right decision for her. Though I miss her like crazy." Rachel gives me what I interpret as an appreciative once-over. "And then there's you."

"And then there's me." It's silly to repeat the phrase, but it's all I can do while my heart skips a beat. Did Laura talk to Rachel about me?

"She told me about that kiss, by the way." Rachel is beaming a big smile at me now, then just rambles on. "Either way, I've heard her mention the name Tess over the phone so many times, I just had to come to Nelson and see for myself."

"She, er, has mentioned me?" My cheeks are starting to heat up.

"Of course she has. What else is she going talk about? The new movie in the multiplex and the new art show at the Nelson Museum of Modern Art?" Rachel narrows her eyes. "She has feelings for you, Tess. That's clear as day. I already knew that before I arrived here, and my suspicions have only been confirmed, but she needs time. It's only natural for her to be afraid. Tracy was a perfectly nice woman when they met. I was Laura's maid of honor at their wedding, for Christ's sake. I signed my name on a goddamned piece of paper to approve their union."

"We're friends." I find myself repeating the phrase over and over again. It's starting to get old.

"She may have feelings for you, but you might have to be friends for quite some time before anything else can happen. You're going to have to win her trust and then some. So she'd better be worth the wait to you."

Rachel is starting to make me feel as though I'm auditioning for the part of Laura's girlfriend. "I get it," is say a tad defensively. "Trust me, I get it."

"I didn't mean to give you a speech, Tess. Laura is strong, but we all have a breaking point. I'm not sure how much more she can take."

"My ears were ringing so loudly, I just had to come over and break up this let's-discuss-Laura party," Laura says.

I'd been so engaged in conversation with Rachel, that I didn't see her approach.

"We're only looking out for you." Rachel wraps an arm around Laura's shoulder and pulls her close. This is the most at ease I've seen Laura, when she's around Rachel.

Laura gives a sheepish smile, then looks over to the chairs where her parents are sitting. "I'd better go do this," she says. "Get it over with." She eyes my glass of wine longingly.

Rachel doesn't say anything, though she must see this as well.

"Need some liquid courage?" I ask.

"You know what?" Laura says. "Yes, I do. Today of all days, I do."

I offer her my glass, but before she can take it, Rachel says, "Are you sure?"

Laura just nods, takes the glass and brings it to her lips. After she's taken a sip, she asks, "Can I hold on to this?"

"Sure."

"Here I go," she says, and walks off. Before she reaches her parents, she's accosted by a few people saying their goodbyes.

"I hope this ends well." Rachel glances at Laura, then looks back at me. "I was with her on the night Tracy died. We'd been out and, over a few drinks—a few too many perhaps—she talked about leaving Tracy for the first time. She'd needed a lot of liquid courage for that as well. Then… she didn't need to leave her anymore."

"I can't imagine what that must have felt like."

"Honestly, to me, it felt like a relief," Rachel says. "Maybe I'm not supposed to say that about a woman who died well before her time, but by God, what she put Laura through. And who knows what it would have taken Laura to actually leave her? Tracy might have ended up killing *her* first."

I'm taken aback by Rachel's forwardness. "It was a complex situation."

Rachel shakes her head vehemently. "There was nothing complex about it. After they married, Tracy turned into a controlling, abusive monster. She terrorized Laura. Scolded her for the smallest things. She beat her, Tess. Broke one of her ribs one day. The woman was a two-faced psychopath. Maybe nobody else knows, but I do."

I see my mother coming over, and clear my throat to warn Rachel. A change of subject is required pronto.

"Hey, hon," Mom says. "We're going to take off. Aunt Margaret is minding the kids and you know she can only handle them in small doses. Megan and Scott will stick around for a while."

I introduce her to Rachel, who promptly gets an invitation to dinner—not to be refused—while my gaze wanders to Laura. She's talking to Elizabeth Jansen, Milly's oldest friend in Nelson, so she might not make it over to her parents in a good long while. The glass of wine I gave her is empty now.

Make them wait, I think. Laura waited long enough.

LAURA

W hen I finally reach my parents, I've had another refill of wine, and after so many months without a drop of alcohol, I've almost finished my second glass of the day. I haven't eaten much; my appetite went as soon as the black sedan showed up. So the alcohol has gone straight to my head, which I consider a good thing. I don't feel much like doing this sober.

"You would love a chance to what?" I ask my father, who looks like a fidgety shadow of the mighty Pastor Baker. "I'm giving you a chance to finish that sentence, so there you go."

"Can we speak somewhere privately?" my mother asks.

I want to contest her, just because I can, but quite frankly, I'd much rather have this conversation without Tess and Rachel lurking in the other corner of the room.

"Follow me." I lead them to the patio outside. It's a muggy day and the black blouse I bought for the occasion sticks to my back instantly, as though I've just stepped into a vacuum-sealed room instead of the early Texas summer.

We sit around the table, me with my back to the garden,

though I could use the sight of some greenery and the memories of Aunt Milly it inspires.

"We're glad you called," my father starts. "And we're glad to see you." The thing about my father is that, because of his profession, he can make the biggest bullshit sound like the most genuine words you've ever heard. "Glad to see you're doing well."

Doing well? What a joke.

"I heard you live here now," my mother says. "Is there any particular reason you came here?"

"A relative in need of company and help." I try to keep my voice firm. I could do with another glass of wine. As far as uncomfortable situations go, this one is right up there with being questioned by a police officer after Tracy's death. I don't want to be here, I keep thinking. I don't want to sit here with these people and exchange words with them. It's all too little too late.

I look at neither of them, but just stare through the window inside. I can make out Rachel and Tess, though I can't see their features clearly. Then, I realize that I don't have to have this conversation. I can walk away any time.

"We should have come to your wedding," my father says then, and it feels like being kicked hard in the gut. Like all life just rushes from me in a wave of pain. "We're sorry about that."

They don't even know Tracy is dead. I sent them a wedding invitation but no notification of my wife's untimely demise. They don't know anything. These people who created me, raised me, and tried to mold me into their image.

"Why did you come here?" I ask.

"She was my sister," my father is quick to say.

"Fat load of good that did her." My nerves have no way out of my system, so I start tapping my heel against the floor.

"I'm almost eighty, Laura, and, lately, I've started to realize that throughout my life I've made a few grave errors." He tries to find my gaze, but I look away. When I glance back at him, however, I see too much of me in that sad, old face. I inherited his eye color, and that dimple in his chin, and a bunch of other features that conspire together to reveal we are related.

My mother remains silent. Maybe they agreed that the pastor would do the talking—for maximum impact.

"Your mother and I are very sorry for casting you out the way we did." His tone is exactly the same as I remember from the endless hours of services I had to sit through as a child. "Times have changed. We even have some gay folks in our congregation these days."

"Oh really?" I stare him hard in the face. "And what did you tell them? You're very welcome here. Our daughter is a lesbian. We were too stupid and cold-hearted to accept her, but we'd like to make up for that by embracing you into the bosom of our church."

"Laura, we know what we did was wrong," my father again. "We're not here to ask for your forgiveness, because we know that's too much to ask. We're here to try and make a start of, perhaps, rebuilding our relationship with you. Before it's too late."

"You mean before you die?" Nerves are quickly transforming into anger. "It's been fifteen years. And *I* called *you*. I'm not buying any of this. If Aunt Milly hadn't died, you wouldn't even be here."

My dad utters a sigh, while my Mom finally speaks. "Which one is your wife?" she asks, her voice as icy as ever. "The tall blond or the short African-American?"

That's it. I've had it. I push my chair back and stand up. "I would like you both to leave now."

"Laura, come on." I witness how my father gives my mother a scolding look. At least now I know which one of the two instigated their trip here. "Let's talk a little longer. We came all this way."

"Oh, the sacrifices you've made for me." I don't care that I'm raising my voice. I don't care who hears what I have to say. I look at my mother. "Neither one of them is my wife. My wife is dead. And please stop pretending you care one iota. I will never have a relationship with you. Why would I spend even a second of my life considering whether to forgive you, my parents, the people who hurt me the most in my life. Do you have any idea what it feels like to cease to exist for your own kin? Every Christmas, every Thanksgiving, every birthday, every single year, was never a celebration for me, just a brutal reminder of how cruel you were. Yet, for the first few years, every single time, I had hope. Foolish, ridiculous hope that you'd see past your bigotry. But it never happened. Not a word. Nothing in fifteen years. Do you have any idea what that does to a person?"

"Laura." A voice comes from behind me.

"You're fifteen years too late, *Daddy*," I say.

"Laura." I feel a hand on my shoulder. I look to my right. It's Rachel, Tess right behind her. "Come on, let's go inside," Rachel says.

I look at my parents' flabbergasted faces one more time— and some part of me hopes it's the last time I see them—then let Rachel coax me inside, into the room I use as my office.

"Are you all right?" Tess is there as well, of course.

My breath is coming quickly, my pulse is pounding. "I lost it when my mother asked which one of you was my wife." Whereas it enraged me before, the statement now sounds so ludicrous, I burst out into a silly giggle. When I come to, I say, "It was just such blatant evidence of how they know absolutely nothing about me. Of how family is not always who you're born to, but who loves you." I look at Rachel, then at Tess. I love them both in my own way. "I don't have many people left, but I have you two." Emotions are quickly starting to catch up with me and my eyes are getting itchy.

"You will always have me," Rachel says as she grabs my hand.

I glance at Tess, who stands there looking as though she doesn't know what to do. But she doesn't have to say or do anything, I know she has my back. Sometimes, you just know. Even when the most horrible things have happened to you, and the person you loved most in the world, the person you were so in love with that you married her, tried to take the last speck of your dignity with her fists. Even then, you can still know. Because I know now, while Rachel holds my hand, and I stare into Tess's eyes, I know she won't hurt me.

"Shall I guide them off the premises?" Rachel asks. "Tell them to never return?"

"Please do." I take a deep breath, happy to have kept my tears at bay. I know I'll have to let them out at some point, but now is not the time.

"I'll get the remaining people to leave, okay?" Tess says.

I nod, and look her over again. She even looks beautiful in funeral clothes. "Thank you, Tess." I reach out my hand and grab for hers. The few times I've held her hands I always noticed how impossibly soft they were—as though made for the single purpose of offering solace and bringing joy.

Tess looks at our joined hands, then looks up. "Maybe a glass of wine too many?" She gives the smallest of smiles, but no matter how small, it says enough.

"Maybe, but I didn't say anything they didn't fully deserve to hear."

"No doubt." The grip of Tess's fingers around mine intensifies. "I'll be right back. Sit down for a bit."

"Okay." I watch her leave the room and I sit down at my desk. I take the sketch pad that I always have lying around and start drawing. I sketch what is in my heart. The result is a loose-lined portrait of Tess.

"Why don't you move here as well?" I ask Rachel. She's on a late-night flight back to Chicago and I already know the house will feel so empty without her, despite her only having stayed here a couple of nights.

"Because the city wouldn't be the same without me. It might very well be in shambles already right now," she jokes.

"I don't know if I'll ever come back, Rach." I sip from my cup of green tea. Two glasses of red wine at the funeral were enough to get me back on the alcohol-free path.

"I don't think you should." Rachel is doing her best to finish the remaining bottles of wine from the reception. "I think you can thrive here, Laura. I really do."

"Could it be, when you say that, you are referring to a lady called Tess?"

"You know I am." Rachel looks at me over the rim of her glass. "You told her about Tracy, which leads me to believe that you must really trust her. That you opened up to her."

I ponder this, though I don't even need to think about it anymore. "I do trust her."

"That's the start, Laura. That's a really strong foundation." Rachel looks at me with a bit of a twinkle in her eyes. "I also quizzed and lectured her. My best-friend conclusion is that I approve."

"You what?" At the reception, I as good as crashed a conversation they were having about me, so it hardly comes as a surprise. Though I feel I need to feign indignation a little.

"Oh come on, Laura. Did you really think we weren't going to talk about you? Besides, I wouldn't be doing my duty if I wasn't looking out for you."

"Did you exchange phone numbers so you can discuss my future progress as well?"

Rachel smiles that toothy smile of hers. "We did exchange

contact information, but I don't need progress reports from anyone else but you." She sets her glass on the table. "But on a more serious note, Laura, how do you feel, now that you've seen your parents again and, after what happened?"

"Strangely relieved." I lay awake until the early morning thinking about the effect of my parents' visit and my outburst. "Like a weight has been lifted off my shoulders. I hadn't seen them in so long and made a shitload of automatic assumptions, and now I can stop doing that. I can stop wondering. I've seen them. They're two old people. My father might have felt a tad sorry, but my mother certainly didn't. As far as I can remember, she has never been the most affectionate woman, but all I saw when I looked at her was cold indifference. Like she didn't care what my response would be. In a way, that makes it easier."

Rachel nods, drinks more wine. "Do you think your father was serious about restoring the relationship?"

"I don't know. He sounded sincere, but that doesn't mean anything. In the end, it doesn't matter what he wants, because I don't want a relationship with them. I'm done with them—have been for a very long time. I may never be completely rid of them. I don't think that's possible, but I'm a different person now. I know that I don't need them. I've been through enough without them."

Rachel looks at the clock. "My taxi will be here soon."

"I know."

"There's one more thing I'd like to discuss."

"Better hurry then."

"Are you going to give Tess a chance?" She narrows her eyes and scans my face.

I look away for an instant, then slowly start nodding.

24

TESS

I meet Laura for coffee the day after Rachel leaves. I haven't seen her since the reception—since she grabbed my hand in her office.

"I get to pick up my kitten today," she says. "Myriam just called."

"Exciting." Somehow, I can't seem to inject any excitement into my voice though, and my words sound flat and unenthusiastic.

"What's wrong?" Laura asks, and I see genuine concern in her eyes.

"Just, er... some things Rachel said, I guess."

"Like what?" Laura shuffles nervously in her chair.

"She didn't tell you?"

"She told me that she quizzed you and subsequently gave her best-friend stamp of approval." Laura quirks up her eyebrows twice in quick succession. I have no idea what her body language is supposed to suggest. Maybe she's nervous. Well, so am I.

"Approval for what exactly?" I distinctly remember feeling like I was being put to the test by Rachel. I'd be mortified if

Megan grilled Laura like that. Then again, I probably don't need the amount of mother-hen protection that Laura does.

"Look, Tess, after that, er, thing with my parents," Laura reaches for her bag on the floor. "After you left the room, I drew this." She opens up her sketch pad and thrusts it in my direction.

When I look at what she drew, I see me. "That's beautiful." I find her gaze. "Why did you draw that?"

"Because I had a rare moment of being able to look past all the bullshit and grief in my life, and what I saw was you."

"And now? What do you see now?"

"I'm sitting across from you." Laura gives a nervous chuckle. "So I'm seeing you now as well."

I clear my throat. "Rachel said some things that made me think. Nothing that I didn't know yet, I guess. But there were definitely some mixed signals in there. I mean, by now everything is one big mixed signal in my head. She told me that you'd mentioned me many times and that she could clearly see you had feelings for me, but she also told me that my patience would need to be tested for quite some time longer. And I have patience, Laura, because I care for you. But you told me explicitly not to wait for you, though waiting for you is exactly what I'm doing. And this confusion is starting to do my head in. I'm doing my best to not put any pressure on you, because I know it's unfair, but what I'm trying to say is that I have feelings too."

"I know that. And for the record, I don't feel pressured." Laura goes silent for a few seconds, while my heart thunders in my chest. Did I overstep? "But I don't really know if I can tell you to wait for me if I have no idea how long. There's a war raging inside here too, Tess." She taps a finger against her temple. "I care greatly for you too. I would love to go out with you, but I'm so afraid of what it might do to me. I'm also afraid of putting myself out there. And that's just the emotional part. Physically I, er, I really don't know if I'm ready for any of that."

She stares into her tea. "I guess I don't want to fuck it up. Your friendship means too much to me and it's not something I can afford to lose."

"You will never lose me, Laura." I know it's the wrong thing to say as soon as the words come out of my mouth.

Laura gives me a skeptical look. "Of course I will. You have a good and big heart, Tess. I know that much. But if we go out and it doesn't feel right or something happens or gets said and it ends badly, not even you could get past that."

"But what could possibly happen?" My voice sounds way too exasperated.

"I know it might be hard for you to wrap your head around this. I totally get that. I know I'm not easy to deal with, especially when it comes to this... to having feelings for someone. But certain things happened to me that I can't even say out loud. Things I'm so ashamed of I couldn't even tell Rachel. I came to Nelson to heal. That has always been my first and foremost objective. And then I met you, and you're so wonderful, but that doesn't change what happened to me. I know very well I sound like a broken record when I endlessly repeat that I need time, and that must be very frustrating for you, but it is how it is. This healing process I need to go through can't be rushed. As much as I would like to rush it, and be ready to go out with you, I just... can't."

"I'm sorry, Laura. I *did* pressure you." I don't even know where to look, though Laura did just sound a tad patronizing.

"No, it's fine. It's important for us to talk about this. I really need you to know how I feel about you. I just... need some more time." Laura's words are coming faster now. "Like you said after I tried to kiss you, I want it to be the right time for us too."

"But *you* kissed *me*, Laura. You drew that portrait of me. How should I interpret that?"

Laura buries her head in her hands briefly. "I know," she

mumbles from behind her hands. "I'm sorry." She lets her hands fall away. "But to date you, I would need to be completely open with you, and I have no idea how to do that. I can't repeat the things Tracy said to me and turned me into this... damaged person I am today."

"You don't have to tell me anything." I reach for Laura's hand on the table. "I will gladly wait for you, just tell me I have a chance."

Laura tries to look me in the eyes, her gaze skittering away and back to me. "Of course you have a chance. I just don't know how to give it to you."

"It doesn't matter." As far as romantic declarations of intent go, this one is very stunted and rather limited, but it makes me hopeful nonetheless. "That's all I need to know."

"I just need to ask one more thing of you." Laura's playing with my fingers now, letting them fall between hers on the table.

"Anything."

"Don't ask me out. I will ask you when I'm ready." She looks at me from under her lashes.

"Deal." I close my fingers around hers.

"One more thing." Her gaze softens. "Where can I find a litter tray and a food bowl for my kitten?"

25

LAURA

"When do you think I'll be ready?" I ask Socks, my brand new housemate. He's mostly ginger, but his paws are white. His ears perk up a little at the sound of my voice, but not a whole lot. I had believed it would take him much longer to get used to his new surroundings but a few hours after I brought him home, he was already purring on the sofa. "Do you remember that pretty lady who was with me when I picked you up? She's the one I'm talking about." I scratch Socks under his chin and he purrs loudly again. His furry presence effortlessly lifts my spirit.

It's been a few days since Tess and I talked at Mary's. Over the phone, I told Rachel about what she'd said, but she only confirmed Tess's words: *she will wait for you.*

"Why would she, though?" I ask Socks, who turns onto his back and smacks his tiny paws against my hand while I rub his stomach. "Why would she wait for me?"

Though Tess clearly stated that she didn't want to pressure me, having the conversation equaled applying pressure. I fully understand why she said the things she said. But, as a consequence, I am feeling the pressure. The ball's in my court. I will ask her out when I'm ready—whenever that will be.

Then the bell rings, startling Socks. He rolls over and stands with his little ears fully perked up now.

"Shall we see who that is, little fella?" I pick him up and cradle him in my arms. He really couldn't be a more perfect kitten. He seems to love humans as much as we adore cats.

I open the door and see the postman. "Special delivery for you, Miss Baker. Please sign here."

"I told you before, Gunther. The name's Laura." I shoot him a grin as I take the pen he offers. I get a lot of mock-ups and other graphic design samples delivered, so we've become acquainted enough to be on a first-name basis.

"Sure thing, Laura," he says the exact same thing he always says, but always goes back to Miss Baker at his next visit.

He hands me the package, which is just an envelope. At first I think it's a bill I forgot to pay, but when I look at the label I see it's from Mr. Caan, the town lawyer.

"Must be something to do with Aunt Milly," I tell Socks, as I realize that it didn't take me very long to pick up the habit of talking to my pet out loud.

I put Socks on the sofa and he starts mewling immediately. He's such a sucker for affection—at night he sleeps on the pillow, right next to my head. "I thought it was your nap time." I give him a few quick scratches on the top of his head which seem to satisfy him. "You're such an attention whore."

Inadvertently, he makes me smile. He lies down with his head on his paws but doesn't close his eyes, as though he wants to keep tabs on what I'm doing.

I sit down next to Socks and open the envelope. Inside, I find a letter from Mr. Caan's office and the envelope Aunt Milly asked me to drop off there not long after I moved to Nelson.

The letter says that Millicent Johnson wanted me to receive

this letter two weeks after she passed away, which reminds me that it has been two weeks already.

I tear it open and read. It's written in minuscule handwriting, the lines of the words jagged, as though written with a shaky hand. The ink color changes in the middle of the page. It must have taken her a while to get this down on paper.

Dearest Laura,

Some things are better said in a letter. I feel my time here is quickly coming to an end and I want you to know two things. These are my beliefs. They are things I didn't feel entirely comfortable talking to you about in person, but they need to be said.

1) My brother, your father, is not worth one single minute of agony. I have made my peace with the fact that he and I are no longer on speaking terms (also because of someone I loved!) a very long time ago. This may be harder for you but as you get older, it will get easier. I want you to know this. You will care less and less until you've cut that man out of your heart completely. I truly wish you can accomplish this because there is nothing wrong with you, Laura. It's all him and Phyllis. They've brainwashed themselves and I'm sure they're convinced that, through some twisted logic, they're doing good by following God's word. But it's not you who is not worthy of them, it's they who are not worthy of you. You are a beautiful person, and I can surely attest to that, and it's THEIR incomprehensible, giant loss.

2) This one is harder for me to put into words, but I will try. I don't have children, but I consider you one of my own. I want for you what I would want for any of my children. I want you to be happy. Though I know that's hard after everything that has happened to you, you must try. This may require you to take a leap of faith, but I'm convinced that you'll know when the time is right. Healing is important, but you can't let your life pass you by. You have so much more life left to live and I, for one, refuse to believe that what happened to you decreases your chances at happiness. Take the leap, dear Laura. Do it for yourself. You deserve it.

All my love,

Aunt Milly

I stare at the letter for a long time. I gave Aunt Milly very broad strokes of what happened. She knew about the accident, but not about the abuse. The way it's written, however, feels as though she looked straight into my soul and knew everything. And then proceeded to tell me exactly what I needed to hear. I read the letter a few more times, let the words sink in deeper and deeper with every pass, until I can't ignore its message any longer. I'm taking the leap. The time is right.

26

TESS

"I couldn't believe it when you called." I still can't believe it. "Are we still officially calling this a date, Miss Laura Baker?" Below my chair, Laura's kitten pushes himself against my shins time after time.

"It's a date," Laura confirms. When she called me two days ago to ask me out, no hesitation in her voice at all, she said that it would have to be at her house because she couldn't bear to leave Socks alone yet.

"Wine?" she asks. She has dressed up in a white blouse, a step up from her usual t-shirts.

"I don't have to drink," I reply. Though I'm much more nervous than I thought I would be and I could do with a drop.

"I bought it especially for you," she insists. "I may have a tiny sip myself." She pours me a glass, then sits. "Why is this so nerve-racking? We've known each other for months now."

"Because we're calling it a date," I say, knowing exactly how she feels.

Laura busies herself with pouring us each a glass of water. I relent and pick up the kitten.

"He needs a lot of attention," Laura says. "But he'll get tired soon enough."

Socks purrs like crazy and I can't help but press him against my chest. After I've put him back down, I search for Laura's gaze, and hold it for an instant. "I'm nervous too," I admit.

"First date jitters. That's normal, right?" Laura stands again.

"Laura, please, just sit down for a second."

"We should have done this at a restaurant," she says, a gasp in her voice.

"I don't care if we have takeaway pizza. I didn't come here for the food." My heart's already thudding in my chest, and the evening has just begun. I don't feel the slightest pang of hunger —except for Laura. Though I'm getting way ahead of myself again.

"I'm truly relieved you have such low gastronomical expectations." Laura manages a smile. "I'm not exactly a domestic goddess."

"My mother still cooks most of my meals," I say with a giggle.

"She could have cooked for us," Laura jokes.

"She would have in a heartbeat if you'd asked her."

"But we'd have a chaperone."

"And we're a little too advanced in age for that." The moment of banter brings a smile to both our faces. "I'm really happy to be here, Laura." I broaden my smile, hoping to convey the warmth I feel inside.

"I took the leap," she says cryptically. "Aunt Milly made me do it."

"Aunt Milly?" Is she seeing ghosts now?

"She left me a letter. It got delivered two days ago. The first thing I did after reading it was call you."

"Must have been some letter."

"Short, but very powerful."

"It was Aunt Milly who brought you here and now she got

you to 'take the leap' so to speak. Looks like I owe your aunt a lot."

"You and me both. Who knows where I would have ended up if not in Nelson?"

"Maybe in cowgirl Sherry's claws somewhere. She'd be reading you poetry under the stars."

"Are you sad she never got to perform a private poetry slam for you?" Laura asks.

"Is that a euphemism?" I ask, snickering, as I feel the nerves drain out of me.

"No." Laura shakes her head. "Or I guess it could be."

"I'm not the slightest bit sad, Laura." She seems more relaxed as well.

"I was jealous, you know? I practically pushed you into her arms, but I was so jealous."

Confession time already. I like what I'm hearing very much. "That's interesting." I can't keep the glee out of my voice.

Laura pauses, then speaks. "So, as this is our first real date, we should get to know each other better." She sounds very official all of a sudden. "We should tell each other things we don't know about each other yet."

"Okay... But that sounded as though you were reading it from a piece of paper and, unsuccessfully I might add, rehearsed that line in front of the mirror all afternoon."

"I haven't dated in a long time. I don't really know what to do."

I suppress the urge to rush to her for a hug. "You don't have to do anything. You've done the hard work already. You picked up the phone and called me. From here on out, it'll be a walk in the park."

She takes a deep breath. "Let's start again. We can begin by you giving me a hand in the kitchen, for example. But, I do have one rule. I absolutely do want us to get to know each other better, but no heavy subjects tonight. I don't want to talk about my parents or about Tracy. This is a new beginning for me and I don't want to look back."

"Deal. So… what should I expect when I follow you into the kitchen?"

"A battlefield," Laura says and gets up to show me.

———

WE'VE MOVED to the sofa where, after dinner, Socks has taken up residence on Laura's lap. I crave for her fingers to stroke me the way they do him. But, truth be told, I'm already so elated just to be sitting here with her.

"Tell me your happiest memory," she asks then. The top button of her blouse has come loose a while ago, but I haven't told her.

"Oh no," I groan. "Ask me a less philosophical question."

"Okay." Her eyes glint with mischief. "As you can see I'm trapped under something tiny and I'm in the mood for a small glass of wine. Would you pour me one, please?"

"The lady shall be served pronto." I know where she keeps the wine glasses, so I get her one and fill it halfway.

"Here you go." When I pass her the glass, I linger in her personal space, and gaze deep into her blue eyes. "At your service."

"Thanks." She shuffles her weight around enough for Socks to lift his head and utter an offended high-pitched meow. "Apologies, my lord," she says. "Just trying to get comfortable under your crushing weight."

"He's really taken to you." I sit back down. I'll have to wait for my moment, and it may not happen tonight, but I want that kiss she instigated a few weeks ago. "I can see why."

She draws her lips into a slow smile, takes a sip, looks at me, and asks, "Why do you like me so much, Tess?"

"Quite frankly, because you're the only other single lesbian in Nelson and I'm sick and tired of being alone." Goodness me. Why did I ruin this moment with a stupid joke? It was going so well. God knows what it took Laura to ask me that question.

But she seems unfazed by my silliness and just says, "Exactly what I thought."

"I can spell it out for you, if you'd like." I look at her while she sips from her wine.

She shakes her head. "No need. I'm not that insecure." She sits up, takes another sip and puts her glass down. "Sorry, Mister, I'm going to put you here for a bit." She moves Socks off her lap and puts him on a pillow next to her. Then she shuffles to the edge of the couch, looks at her hands for an instant, before reaching for mine.

"You're a country girl," she says, "how come your hands are so impossibly soft?"

My heart is thudding wildly. There's a question I hadn't expected. "Gloves, I guess," I mutter, while moving as close to Laura as I can without our knees touching.

She lifts my hands to her face and stares at them, as though considering my response, then presses a kiss to the back of each one. "Thank you for waiting," she whispers.

My throat has gone very dry, but I need to say this. "It didn't feel like waiting. When you know, you know."

This brings a smile to her face. "When did you know?"

When I accidentally cornered you in the supermarket, I want to say, but this is no time for more silliness. "A long time ago." It's hard to pinpoint the exact moment. Like so many things in life, it was a gradual process. In the beginning, it manifested itself as the unshakable desire to spend as much time with her as possible. Then the flirting started, followed by Laura Baker becoming a permanent fixture in my mind.

"Well then." Laura bites her bottom lip, sucks it into her mouth. "Time to finish what I started two weeks ago." She doesn't close her eyes when she leans in, slants her head, and brings her lips to mine.

I taste wine and smell her flowery perfume. Our hands are still intertwined. Our lips are barely touching, but my whole body is coming alive—as though it's cheering for me. I try to let Laura set the pace for as long as I can control myself. Her lips linger longer, are starting to open more and then the tip of her tongue slips in. Our hands are clasped together and our mouths are exploring each other and my heart is about to burst out of my chest. I feel the kiss everywhere, I feel my ears glow red and my cheeks flush and my toes curl with anticipation, but it's so much more than just an added physical connection. I know what Laura had to overcome to do this—though, I suspect, I don't know half of it yet—and if Aunt Milly were still alive, I'd be writing her a thank-you letter first thing in the morning.

Laura lets my hands slip from hers and grabs me by the back of the neck, pulling me closer. Our tongues venture farther, deeper, and the goosebumps that the initial, careful pecks instigated turn into a red hot flame licking over my skin. I haven't been touched in a long time and my unmet desires are starting to catch up with me.

I push her down onto the sofa, our chests meeting in a soft crash, her hands all tangled up in my hair. When we finally break from the kiss, I need to catch my breath because of the emotional intensity of it.

Our eyes meet. My lipstick has been smeared all over Laura's lips and another button of her blouse has come undone.

In a flash, she pulls me close again, on top of her this time, and we kiss again and again, our tongues now freely dancing in each other's mouths. She sucks my bottom lip into her mouth, and I latch onto hers with my teeth. It's glorious and beautiful and, surely, the gateway to all the things I want to do with

Laura, but I pace myself—I really try—and let her control what happens next.

The only noise around us is the sound of our lips coming together or apart, though I may also hear my heart beat in my ears, and feel the wetness gathering between my legs. This time, when we break from our kiss, I let my lips trail down her chin to her neck, and kiss her there. And I must have lost myself for a few seconds, because next thing I know I'm kissing the hollow of her neck and am peppering kisses where her blouse has come open.

"Tess, Tess, please." Laura's hands are on the side of my head, breaking the spell I was under. "Come here for a minute."

I crawl upward while my skin sings with desire. "Too much, too soon?" I ask.

"I want you, Tess. I need you to know that. But we're going to have to take this slow."

"No problem." I hope my smile is understanding and not too leery.

"We can kiss all you like, though." Laura doesn't seem worried, and she surely has a sparkle in her eyes.

I push myself up more, until I'm on my knees next to her. I plant my hands behind her shoulders and slip one knee over her lap. "Kissing it is." I look down at her, at that smile that's becoming more confident by the minute. "And remember what I told you a while ago," I say, before bowing down to kiss her again. "I'm not one to put out on the first date, anyway."

We both burst out into a giggle and when our lips meet this time, there's still desire running through my veins, saturating every cell of my being, but it's accompanied by a happiness, a deeply satisfying sense of contentment, that I haven't encountered in years.

27

LAURA

I see no way of telling Tess that the sex Tracy and I had was most likely one of the main reasons I couldn't bear to walk away from her. Not even after I had to spend three nights in the hospital with a broken rib and a punctured lung.

"She fell down the stairs," Tracy told her family and our friends who came to visit, "you know how clumsy Laura can be." Then she'd sit by the side of my bed and hold my hand while she looked into my eyes with such sorrow, sporting such a genuine display of regret that, even though my broken bones had only just begun to heal, I was ready to forgive her already. Because she had made a mistake. An unfortunate, inexcusable mistake in a fit of rage that was uncharacteristic for her. She didn't know what had come over her. It would surely never happen again, because she loved me so much and how could she deliberately want to hurt the person she loved most in the world? She would see a therapist, get that crooked wiring in her brain fixed as soon as possible.

At first, I believed her. Because that really wasn't the Tracy I knew, the Tracy who looked into my eyes and didn't even need to say anything because I could see in her fierce, strong glance how much she adored me. The woman whose face had contorted into an angry grimace when she shoved me onto the floor and let her shoe land against my ribcage, was not the deliriously happy smiling woman I had married two short months earlier. This was surely someone else.

When I was released from the hospital, Tracy waited on me hand and foot. She was tall and strong and carried me from the bed to the sofa, made me endless cups of tea and prepared me a home-cooked dinner every night. As soon as the pain started to recede and I was up to it, she lay next to me in bed and ran her fingers over my skin—those fingers that could ball into a fist in a split second—while she had that glint in her eyes which I couldn't resist. And when she spread my legs and went down on me, I always—even then—came with such obliterating force that, for a moment, I could forget the ugly version of her that existed. Because sex with Tracy was my weakness and the chemistry between us was palpable in the air. It consumed me so much that I lost my perspective—that I believed her when she said she would rather take her own life than ever hurt me again. Until she did.

Near the end, I could so easily predict when the cycle of inflicting pain, extreme care and bottomless apologies had come full circle again. I could see it in her glance as well. And still, I didn't leave. It's the not being able to walk away part that I can't forgive myself for. If I had, she'd still be alive. I wouldn't have the blood of another human being on my hands.

I stand in front of the mirror, getting ready for my fourth 'official' date with Tess and ask myself whether I'm ready for this. But it's the same woman staring back at me as when I first arrived, as when Tess came over for the first date, the second, and the third. I guess I won't know until I actually try, even though I don't know how I can allow another person to touch me like that. Because, with Tracy, there was always a price to pay in the end. Even though I know that Tess is not Tracy, some thought patterns are so persistent not even time and distance can erase them.

When the bell rings, I take a deep breath. Tess and I have kissed, and fondled, and whispered sweet nothings in each other's ear, but every time the tension was about to rise to boiling point, I had to stop her. I tried not to so very hard, but as soon as my brain—and my fear—started to take over, I knew I had to step in. I knew I wasn't ready.

But I can't keep on blowing her off like that, not because I think her patience will run out, but because I want to break the pattern, I want to bust through my defenses and give myself to Tess, I want to undo Tracy's grasp on me. It's time.

"Hey," Tess says. She's wearing the same dress she wore when she took me to her land on the outskirts of Nelson, and she's holding up a bunch of flowers. "Happy fourth date." She hands me the flowers and I melt a little inside. On our first date, when I asked her why she liked me so much and she blew me off with a quick quip, I had really wanted her to tell me, though I know that some things don't need to be said. Some things are just obvious.

"Thank you." I take the flowers and hold them in one hand while I pull her inside with the other. As usual, Socks is mewling with excitement at our feet.

As has become the habit, a gentle peck swiftly turns into a frenzied lip-lock and, before I know it, Tess has me gasping for air again. And then, seemingly out of nowhere, the thoughts slam back into my brain with unstoppable force. *What do you think you're doing? Have you lost your mind? Remember last time you let someone kiss you like that?*

I try to ignore them, hold them at bay as best I can, but it's not working, and my lips stiffen on Tess's mouth. "We should talk," I say, because, again, I realize this is not just something we can kiss away. This is something we're going to have to deal with together.

"I like what you've had to say so far." Tess gives me a crooked grin and pulls me close again.

Before she can shut me up with her lips on mine, I say, "No, we should really talk. I need to tell you something."

"Okay." If Tess is disappointed, no signs of it show on her face. "Of course." Every time I do this to her, I can't help but wonder when I will reach the bottom of her well of patience.

We go into the living room and sit. The ceiling fan is whirring. I pour us both a glass of red wine from a bottle I opened an hour ago.

We chit-chat for a while, which is always easy for us to do. She tells me about the prospective buyer who came to check out the last of the ranch's livestock today, and couldn't believe he'd have to do business with a woman. I tell her about a big job I landed today with the county—all thanks to my re-design of *The Nelson Ledger*.

"How's your drawing arm?" she asks, and runs a finger over it as though she can examine it that way.

"Almost as good as new." Although Tracy was way too smart to ever injure my 'money arm' as she called it, it's ironic that the body part she never hurt acted up the most after she was gone.

"I'm so happy to hear that." I can hear in Tess's voice how happy she is for me and I can't wait to make a morning-after drawing of her. Tess Douglas in my bed after a night of love. It's all I want. I can see how it would start, and I yearn for that post-orgasmic haze, but it's the middle part—the action bit— that I have problems with.

"Look, er, Tess," I begin, my voice already shaky. "You might wonder whether Tracy ever hurt me in, er, the bedroom." I avoid Tess's glance, stare at my hands instead. "She didn't. On the contrary. In bed is where we made up." I draw in a deep breath, exhale slowly. "I guess that's what screws with my head the most. Why taking the next step with you is so hard.

Because it reminds me of what it used to mean to me and how, at the same time, it made me feel like the weakest person in the world, but also the most hopeful." I glance up. Tess nods thoughtfully. "I'm by no means saying that we stayed together because the sex was so good." I feel utterly mortified but, strangely, at the same time, relief sets in. "But it was a big part of our dynamic and I just, er, want to warn you that... I don't know. I guess that sums it up. I don't know what it's going to do to me to land in bed with you. For a long time, sex meant something very different to me than it's supposed to mean. Not that there's one true definition or anything." *Entering rambling mode*, a voice in the back of my mind shouts, but I can't stop. As though as long as words are coming from my mouth, I'll be safe. "It's just that, for me, it might not stand for the same beautiful thing that you think it is. I mean, for me right now, as I sit here wanting you so badly, I swear to you, Tess, I want you so much, but I'm so scared right now that it feels more like something I need to get through... if that makes any sense at all."

Tess nods and scrunches her lips together. "First of all, I'm really glad you told me that, because that must have been so hard." She takes my hands in hers. "Second, as long as you feel this way, nothing will happen between us."

"But, no, that's not—" I try to interrupt her, but she holds up her hand.

"Listen to me, Laura. There is simply no way I'm taking someone to bed who isn't one hundred percent ready. I'd constantly be wondering whether what I'm doing is triggering some nasty memory. But—" She holds up a finger. "What I would like to do, tonight or tomorrow or some time next week, is stay the night. Just sleep in the same bed with you. Fall asleep next to you and wake up next to you in the morning. Would that be okay?"

"Yes. More than okay." I look at Tess and conclude I will never know the full extent of how lucky I've been to meet her.

"Slumber party?"

"Yes, Ma'am." I try to mimic her accent but fail miserably.

AFTER AN EVENING of eating frozen pizza, sharing a bottle of wine—my drinking is increasing by the day—and talking while the TV played in the background, we take turns in the bathroom. I go first and when I emerge I find Tess with an exaggerated expression of worry on her face.

"What's wrong?" I crouch down next to her.

"I didn't bring my pajamas. Do you have an old t-shirt I can use?"

"Not an old one. I got rid of all my old clothes before I moved here, but you can borrow one from my vast collection of brand new white tees." I dig my fingers into her thigh to not lose my balance.

"I'm such a tall drink of water, it won't cover much." Her smile is wicked and slow. "Do you think you can handle that?"

"I think I'll be fine." I push myself up, grab a t-shirt from my wardrobe and give it to her.

When Tess is in the bathroom I consider how, earlier, she so deftly defused the situation, but how, because of the early stage of our relationship, some sparks of tension remain. I hop into bed and wait for her there. Of course, Socks has followed me, and has already taken position in his favorite spot on the pillow.

"I may have forgotten to mention that it's a threesome slumber party," I say when Tess exits the bathroom. She wasn't lying when she said my t-shirt would barely cover half her body. The panties she's wearing don't leave much to the imagination either and I'm left to conclude that she must have dressed for what won't be happening tonight.

Tess brings her hands to her side and utters a big sigh.

"Who am I to come between a lesbian and her pussycat?" Then she rushes to bed and slips under the covers with me. Just the weight of her body, and the heat that radiates from it, and the earlier sight of her in her barely-there panties and t-shirt that exposed a sliver of skin of her belly, is enough to send my mind racing into another tailspin of horniness and fear.

"Lights off?" she asks.

"Yep." I find the switch above the bed and the room turns dark. We're both lying on our back and I, for one, am afraid to move a muscle.

"You don't snore, do you?" Tess asks.

"You'll soon find out."

I feel Tess inching closer. "Good night, Laura," she says, and kisses me on the cheek.

28

TESS

Trying to fall asleep next to Laura and in Laura's bed is not an easy task. I've fallen into a restless slumber off and on but, mostly, I'm just waiting for dawn to break through the curtains. It doesn't help that Socks breathes way too heavily for a kitten his age and size—as though every single one of his exhales needs to show utter contentment.

I try not to toss and turn too much, and to keep to my side of the bed. Not only so I don't disturb Laura, but even more so for my own peace of mind. It was a good idea in theory, one I applauded myself for because I didn't feel like driving home with images of what could have been assaulting my brain throughout the journey again, and because it displayed a sensitivity toward Laura that she obviously still needs. But now, lying here next to her, it's more stressful than I could have anticipated. I also wonder if she has slept at all. The last time Laura shared a bed with someone must have been with Tracy, this woman who is dead but still controls a big part of her life —mine as well.

I've been able to resist googling her, because I don't know how it would make Laura feel if I told her that I did. Additionally, I guess I'm afraid of looking at the face of someone who will probably look as ordinary as the next person, someone whose face won't bear any signs of the things she was capable of.

"Are you awake," Laura whispers, startling me.

"Yes. Wide awake, in fact."

"Can't sleep, huh?" Her voice sounds sleep-drenched.

"Strange bed and all that."

"It's my bed and I can't sleep either."

"Well, that's perfectly understandable, of course, what with the foxy lady you have lying next to you."

"Tell me about it." Laura snickers and every single smile or giggle or chuckle I get out of her, always feels like a small victory.

Laura obviously doesn't believe in alarm clocks so I have no idea of the time. The room is totally dark and I can only hear Laura's voice and, when I turn my head, make out her contour under the duvet.

"Do you want to spoon?" she asks, startling me again.

"Sure." Instantly, my pulse picks up speed. "Outer spoon or inner spoon?"

"Inner," she says. Perhaps because the room is bathed in darkness I can make out the inflections in her voice better, but it sounds a little hoarse—it sounds like she desperately wants something.

"Here I come," I announce. I turn on my side and shuffle closer to Laura until my belly touches her backside. I slip one arm under my pillow and curve one over her middle, unsure what to do with my fingers, so I just let them dangle in the space in front of her belly. I leave a tiny gap between our bodies, but she surprises me by pushing herself against me. There's no way I'm getting any more sleep now. "Is that okay?" I ask.

"Perfect." She tilts her head back a bit, and some of her hair

FAR FROM THE WORLD WE KNOW

gets caught in my mouth and tickles my nose, but I don't care. "Will you be able to go back to sleep?"

"No," I say, truthfully, eliciting another giggle from Laura.

"Aren't you exhausted from working on the ranch all day?" she asks, her body convulsing against mine a bit. "All those bulls that need taming and cows that need a-milkin'."

"Hush now, girl," I say in the dirtiest Texas accent I can muster.

"What do you do on the ranch exactly?" she asks.

"Just prance about in my coveralls with a blade of grass between my teeth, whistling and overseeing my land."

"Is it ever possible to have a serious conversation about you?" Laura shifts against me—perhaps I've agitated her?—and, as a result, her ass presses hard into my belly.

"If you catch me at the right time."

"Seriously, though, Tess. I've told you so much about me, and I've gotten to know your family, and the place where you've lived your whole life, yet, sometimes it feels as though I've only just scratched the surface of Tess Douglas."

"I'm just not that interesting." Compared to Laura's, my life so far has been a breeze.

"I hope I'm not prying, but… there must be a reason why you never wanted to leave Nelson. I get that you're close to your family, especially your sister, but isn't falling in love supposed to be stronger than that?"

"What do you mean?" She has me thoroughly confused.

"Have you never fallen in love so hard that it made leaving Nelson a no-brainer?"

"I have. And I have left Nelson. I told you about that. But it didn't work out."

"Come on, Tess. Give me something to work with here. Everyone has a dark secret. What's yours?"

"I've fallen in love; I've had my heart broken; and I've felt very lonely. That's all I can tell you. What you see is what you get with me."

"Okay." She latches on to the arm I have draped over her. "Then I guess it's official. I've never met anyone like you before. Someone who has it so together there's nothing beneath the surface when I scratch." She runs her fingernails over my skin.

"Is that your way of saying I'm boring?" I can't keep a note of indignation out of my voice.

Laura turns on her back. My eyes have grown accustomed to the darkness enough for me to make out her features. "God no. Maybe I was just trying to erase a bit of my own darkness by digging up yours." She's still running her nails over my arm. "Or making sure you really weren't too good to be true." My arm now rests just underneath her breasts.

"What can I say? I'm a good girl." Because she's stroking me, I start skating my fingers over her side in return. My mouth is close to her temple, so I kiss her there.

"Right now, it doesn't feel as though I'm lying in bed with a good girl." Laura clamps her fingers around my arm and, at first, I think she wants me to stop but, instead, she angles her face toward me and kisses me full on the lips. My hand rides up a little, to the bottom of her breast, and I just let it rest there while we kiss.

"I want you," she says, when we break from our kiss.

"Are you sure?" My hand scoots up a little higher.

"Yes," Laura pants, turns fully on her side and presses herself hard against me.

29

LAURA

I press myself hard against Tess, wanting to feel as much of her body against me as possible. Her hand lingering below my breast was what finally pushed me over the edge. The unmistakable effect it was having on me, together with the intimacy of our conversation, all bundled up together like that. She made me feel safe and protected—enough to go through with this right now at least. I want her. And I've stopped asking myself whether it can really be as simple as that. I had to because the answers were driving me crazy.

I need to get out of my head now. I need her to do that to me.

"Hold on," I say when we break from our embrace. I push myself up on one elbow and grab Socks with my free hand. "I'm very sorry, little mister, but you don't want to see this. Time for you to go catch some mice." I put him on the floor, knowing full well that kittens don't take hints like that, but maybe he's hungry—and we'll get lucky.

Though I'm getting lucky already. I can barely see Tess, but I see her eyes shine through the darkness, and I can hear her breath come quick with anticipation, mixed in with my own shallow breaths, because now I've taken this next leap, there's no going back. Yes, I've been afraid, but this has been brewing between us for weeks. This is my time to let go.

I start unbuttoning the very chaste pajama top I put on. I can't bear to feel its fabric on my skin anymore. Everything needs to go. I'm all in. I want her to see and explore all of me—after all, I've allowed her to explore much more of my soul than any other person has in a long time. I let my top slide to the floor. I'm in no position to get the bottoms off as well, but I'm sure Tess will take care of that in due course. Because that's the overall feeling I get when I'm with Tess: that she'll take care of everything from now on. I'm no longer alone. And I want her so badly, my clit is a throbbing mess between my legs already. It pulses like a second heartbeat, pumping desire through my veins.

I flank Tess with my bare chest, pressing a breast against her while I let my finger slide under the hem of the t-shirt she's wearing. Maybe this deal was sealed when she came out of the bathroom before we attempted to sleep. The way she stood there, with her confidence slightly chipped away, and her long, long legs uncovered—her entire stance an invitation I was almost ready to accept.

My finger on her skin is like a drug. Like that first sip of alcohol after a year of abstinence. This tiny gesture, and this tiny surface where our skins meet, gives *me* the confidence to exclaim a resounding, though silent, *yes* to her invitation. I was never shy in the bedroom and I want to show her how I feel, I want her to know that she didn't wait in vain. And that, without her, I would never have been able to build myself up again so quickly in this little town. Though, on the surface I wasn't able to welcome the persistence with which she pursued me, it touched me deep in my heart. It showed me that second chances are real.

She lets my finger continue its slow, upward drift along her belly. The t-shirt rides up along with it and, already, I can't wait to do this in the clear light of day. Light catching in that reddish blond hair of hers, making it look ready to catch on fire any time, like her, like me. To see every inch of her, to share that level of intimacy with another person.

I feel her hand on my back now, tracing its own figure-of-eights, doubling the sensation, multiplying the meeting of our skin. And then I can't bear her being covered by any fabric any longer. I push the t-shirt above her breasts, revealing them to my gaze and I think about how right this is. Though I can't wait to repeat this in daylight, I find it apt for our first time to happen in the darkness of a Nelson night. It symbolizes my own journey from complete ink-black darkness to the little amount of moonlight in my bedroom to whatever light tomorrow, or the day after, or the week after brings.

Tess moves her arms over her head, and I push the t-shirt all the way off her. When her hand returns to my back, it's no longer with a light touch of fingers, but the insistent press of nails against skin. I lean down to kiss her and this is the kiss we've been waiting for. Not just her—though I've teased her long enough—but me also.

Because underneath all the anguish, doubts and hopelessness I've felt for months, there was always a real person lurking. A creature of flesh and blood with too many feelings and cravings and desperations, but a human being nonetheless. And it's what made it harder and easier at the same time. Even in the deepest recesses of my depression, of learning to deal with what I had done, I could always feel my heart beat with a zest for life I couldn't really understand. How could I want to continue living after ending someone else's life? How was that fair? But my heart kept beating like a steady drum, like a cheer, like a rhythmic chant telling me it would be okay. Because what choice did I have but to keep going?

When we break from this kiss, we are both panting, and the

temperature in the room seems to have gone up a notch. I slip half on top of Tess, our breasts meeting, my knee between her legs, getting a little ahead of itself, but I can feel my body taking over now. As though it's saying 'Enough' and locking all my Tracy-related thoughts in a box in the back of my mind, only to be opened again after pleasure has been bestowed. Pleasure and the memory of Tracy can never go together, and my body knows that—every cell of my being knows that.

My lips roam across Tess's neck, pause at the hollow of it, then trace a path down. I glance at her breasts before peppering them with kisses, before closing my lips around her nipple. I grab her other breast with my right hand and let the pure lust riding in my veins take over. I catch her nipple between my teeth, let them sink in until she utters a little yelp, then move on to the other. On a much smaller scale than when I moved to Texas, I'm drawn south again. To where that flimsy pair of underwear is not doing a good job of covering her. I trace a moist path down her belly, along the waistband of her panties, then kiss her through the fabric. I inhale deeply and am floored by how much I've missed another woman's scent. By the primal feeling of it, the acute but simple necessity, by the intimacy it implies.

Tess starts whimpering beneath me, her hands lodging themselves in my hair, while I keep teasing her through the fabric, or perhaps I'm afraid to take the next step—the final one. To look at her there, no barriers between us, will be a point of no return. But I don't want to return to the Laura I was before Tess. Before she climbed into my bed. This divine woman with a heart so big she had room in it to revive mine. Then the moment comes when my fingers push aside the slim panel of her panties and I'm faced with the complete glorious-ness of Tess Douglas. But this is not a moment for looking, or pondering, or even thinking the tiniest thought. This is the moment I let my lips descend upon Tess's sex and taste her, drink her in and, in the process, shed my old skin and grow a new one. Because with Tess, I have no need anymore for the thick skin I lived my life with. The armor I wrapped myself in to keep everyone out. She couldn't be more in now.

I kiss her nether lips, then let my tongue skate along the length of them. And she tastes so earthy, so tangy, so womanly, the sensation connects with my own clit, and I can feel its pulse reverberate through my entire body.

"Oh, Laura," Tess moans, and the croak of her voice connects with my heart, and my heart connects with my tongue, and we've become one being, it feels like, in that moment I unleash my tongue on her clit. It dances and dances, and I suck her into my mouth, play with it there, drink her in, feel her nails pressed into my skull, and think, no, this is not how I want it. This is not the pinnacle of intimacy I crave right now.

So, under soft protest from Tess, I move my face away from between her legs and, my lips smelling of her—an essence I'd like to carry with me for a good long while—I climb up to greet her, to look into her eyes, to see her. I let a hand slip into her panties, and her wetness on my fingers instigates another round of violent throbbing between my own legs, and push one finger inside.

"Oh," she groans, and brings her hands around my neck. "Oh God, Laura." Tess tilts her head back, offering her neck to me, and I kiss it, but only briefly, because I want to see her face. I add another finger and increase my pace, and to be inside of her like that, to give her this pleasure—and take a great deal of my own in the process—is like a giant eraser being swept over the pain in my heart. And I know it's not because of the simple, primal act of being inside her, but because of all that came before since I met her. All the things we've said and done that brought us to this point. To this night I couldn't even have imagined if I had wanted to. No fantasy was able to break through my shield of fear, until now. Now, it's real. This is not a fantasy version of Tess bucking her hips against my fingers, this is the real, formidable, amazing Tess Douglas who saw something in me when we met at the supermarket that day. It doesn't even matter what she saw at that moment, all that matters is that we're here now, together.

She's had her eyes closed since my finger slid inside of her, but she opens them now. She fastens her gaze on mine, her hands still curled around my neck, and it feels as though she's looking straight into my soul. As though, maybe for the very first time, she's seeing the real Laura Baker—the one with all her defenses down. The person I was once and I'm becoming again, with her.

"Oh, Laura, I'm—" Her breath stalls in her throat and her inner walls clamp around my fingers and I'm there with her all the way, as though I can feel her climax shudder through my body as well.

30

TESS

Laura's fingers dig inside me and I can't keep my eyes off her. I look into those mysterious, wounded eyes of hers, wanting so desperately to take away a little of her pain, of her guilt. She narrows her eyes in supreme concentration, and a climax is already engulfing me, spreading its warmth through my flesh, its tingle through my belly, and all I want to do in that moment, when our bodies have come together, is tell her that I love her. Because I think I do. I know I do. I love Laura Baker, no matter how unlovable, and damaged, she considers herself. What is happening in this bed here tonight is nothing short of love.

I draw her close, the aftershocks of the orgasm rippling through me and whisper an appropriate version—for the moment—of *I love you* into her ear. "You're amazing," I say. "Jesus Christ, you're amazing."

Laura lifts up her head and beams me the widest smile. Slowly, she slips her fingers out of me and, already, I want them to return. I don't need time to recover. I've wanted Laura for months and, although there were times I believed this moment would never come, now that it has finally arrived, I never want it to end.

She leans in to kiss me again and I melt into her, holding her close, and I want to touch her like she just touched me, but I still feel I need to ask for explicit permission first. "Do you want me to…" I whisper in her ear.

She pushes herself away from me and smiles down at me. "God, yes," she says. "If you don't I may spontaneously combust." She's so different now, so much more free and relaxed. I can't wait to get those pajama bottoms off her, so I do. They look brand new as well, like all the other items of clothing she owns. It's probably the first time she's worn them. To keep a safe barrier of fabric between us. That didn't work out then.

I pull her close again and when we break from this kiss, I cling to her bottom lip with my teeth, give it a little tug. After I let go, I grin at her, then push her off me so I can be on top.

"Come here," she says, when it's my turn to gaze down at her. I bring my ear close to her lips. "You're beautiful when you come," she says, and it ignites a fresh tingle in my stomach. And a burst of happiness. And the distinct feeling that I'm on top of the world, that nothing or no one will ever harm us ever again. For a brief moment, I can't help but wonder how this is making Laura feel. Her experience can't be the same as mine, but when I look at her, into those sparkling eyes of hers, and her features that have gone soft and become more open, I know it can't be far off.

"Is there anything in particular—" I start to ask.

But she cuts me off, curls her lips into a smile and says, "Stop thinking, Tess. I'm all in. I made the choice. I took the leap. Just be you." Her voice is tender in the night, like music to my ears. And then I do as she tells me.

I let go. Having her fingers inside of me, and coaxing that orgasm from me, was one thing—a spectacular, glorious thing

—but I want, more than anything, to be the cause of Laura's pleasure now. It's a privilege, an honor. A testament to how far we've come. And, also, the finish line to this test of my patience. Yes, I asked her out too soon, and I kissed her a little too passionately too quickly, but I pulled back, adjusted, and waited. I always knew she would be worth it, this moment alone is already more than worth it, although I know, already, without a shadow of a doubt, there will be many more to come.

I kiss her lips, her cheeks, her chin, then, ever so slowly, make my way down. I intend to savor every single second of this, of my most intimate acquaintance with the woman I've fallen in love with. The woman who arrived in my town out of nowhere, and changed everything.

I taste her skin, let my tongue dip into her belly button, which makes her squirm a little. I move one hand to her breast, and realize that I was so focused on my journey down, I neglected them gravely. I kiss my way back up her chest and marvel at the sight in front of me. Laura wasn't lying when she said she was all in, because that's exactly what I see in front of me: a woman ready for anything I'm willing to give.

I let my tongue dart over her nipple while I squeeze her breast. And oh, the softness of another woman's breast in my hand. I can't help it, it makes me think of everything I missed during my years of unintended celibacy. Though, of this I'm certain, Laura was the one to wait for. Having her here now, her body squirming with pleasure at the touch of my tongue, was worth every minute of being single. Of making the choices that I made.

I feast on her nipples, take my time with them, before meandering down again, my lips now on track, no more diversions allowed. I settle between her legs and just gaze in front of me for a few seconds. It's too dark to see much, but I see enough. With Laura, I always saw enough to know I was looking at someone special. This is no exception. I bow down to kiss her there and, instantly, I'm entranced. For the Laura I know to allow me to do this, although I easily, and greedily, allowed her to do the very same thing to me earlier, unleashes a warm blend of love and lust in my flesh, all the way into my bones.

I lick along her lips, avoiding her clit at first, still savoring, until I can't take it anymore. Seeing Laura spread wide in front of me has destroyed the last ounce of patience I had left. I launch a full-on onslaught of licks onto her clit, while I press my fingers deep into the flesh of her behind. I lick as though my life itself depends on it. I lick until Laura goes stiff underneath me and her thighs push against my ears, and she lightly taps me on the head.

I look at her from between her legs, at that big grin on her face and I can't help but break into a wide smile as well. I climb up to meet her anew, because this time, when I look into her eyes, we'll both be a slightly different version of ourselves. We're lovers now and, no matter what happens in the future, nothing or no one can ever take away this night from us.

"You're not so bad yourself," Laura says, which, in the sentimentality department hardly rivals my heartfelt 'you're amazing' from earlier, but Laura and I are so different in so many ways that I can easily recognize it as her way of saying that she cares for me deeply.

31

LAURA

W hen I wake up, my bedroom is brightly lit from the outside. Socks pushes his nose against my cheek, his insistent purr loud in my ear. Next to me, Tess is still sunk into sleep, her breath coming slowly and from a deep place within her.

"She's sleeping the sleep of the utterly satisfied," I whisper to Socks as I pick him up and put him on my chest, which makes him purr even louder. "Keep it down, Socks. You'll wake my lady friend with your enthusiasm."

He gives one of his high-pitched kitten meows. His food bowl is probably empty.

"I'm sorry I had to kick you out of bed, buddy." I pull him a little closer. "It was for your own good." Talking to my kitten, who has wormed his way into my heart from the very first second I laid eyes on him, fills me with a ludicrous sort of happiness. It doesn't matter if I need to kick him off his preferred sleeping pillow to engage in night-time activities, he still seems over the moon at seeing my eyes open in the morning. "We may have to find you alternative sleeping accommodation because that pretty lady over there"—I glance over at

Tess, who doesn't stir—"might make a habit of spending the night."

I try to remember the last time I woke up in the same bed as someone else. After that fatal night with Tracy, I slept on Rachel's sofa for more than a month. She invited me to—purely platonically—share her bed, but I couldn't bear crawling under the covers with another human being, not even with my best friend. The last time I woke up next to someone else like this, was the morning of the day I killed my wife. A day I'll never forget.

I had known from the moment she woke up that it would be one of *those* days. One of walking on egg shells, of my gut gripped by the terror of saying the wrong thing, the one sentence that might provoke her to action. Whereas she would start most days—99 out of a 100—by giving me a big hug in bed, that day she jumped out as soon as she woke up, as though I wasn't even there. It was a Friday, and she often worked from home on Friday and I remember hoping, as I heard the water cascade down in the shower, that she'd be going into the office anyway. Because I always worked from home and, no matter what mood she was in, the energy in the house was always different when she was there as well. I never got as much done as I wanted to because, I realize now, my subconscious was too busy being afraid of what might happen.

"Morning." Next to me the sheets rustle and Tess turns toward me. Her face is all smiles and happiness and joy. "You completely exhausted me last night." She shuffles a little closer, her knee touching my thigh with a little more force than she had probably intended. And I can't help it, but I flinch. I always do.

"I'm sorry," Tess is quick to say. "Let me make that up to you." She ducks under the covers and plants a slew of kisses where her knee landed against my thigh. "Is that better?" she asks when she re-emerges, her eyebrows drawn up, her face serious.

"Come here," I say, pushing all thoughts of Tracy to the back of my mind.

"There's no room for me up there," she jokes. "You already have someone there."

"This little pussycat?" I scratch Socks behind the ears. "He was traumatized during the night by your uncontrollable moaning. I'm just comforting him."

"I guess Socks and I can share your affections." Tess presses herself against my flank and kisses me on the cheek. "Did you sleep okay?"

"I did." I slip an arm underneath her neck and pull her close to me. "Though I was kept awake for a large part of the night by this woman who couldn't keep her hands off me."

"Oh really?" Tess's hand finds it way to my belly. "Like this?" She runs a finger around my belly-button, waking up all the parts of my body that were still slumbering. Her finger travels up and circles a nipple. "Tell Socks it's my turn again," she whispers in my ear, while two of her fingers clasp themselves around my nipple.

"He's not going to be happy," I protest meekly. "Why don't *you* tell him?"

Tess pushes herself up and looks me in the eyes. "I want you, Laura. It doesn't matter that we were up half the night. Having you hasn't stopped my hunger for you. On the contrary. I want you even more now."

I put Socks on the floor and give him a little pat on his tiny body, then pull Tess close for a deep kiss. When she says things like that, I can feel her love for me radiate off her, can see it blazing in her eyes.

"I want you too," I say when we break from our kiss.

Her fingers find my other nipple now and she clamps down hard, making my breath hitch in my throat.

"Good." She squeezes again, then throws the covers off us and trails her lips downward again the way she did last night. She halts at my breasts and swirls her tongue around my nipples and I glance at her mane of wild hair that spreads across my chest and I think, yes, I want this, I want this so badly, but I can't be a hundred percent sure yet. It's impossible. Being in a relationship again is bound to bring back memories, is bound to have me slip back into old, defensive behaviors. And there's the 'unknown' factor. Though Tess is very different from how Tracy was, the enthusiasm of their affections from the very beginning is something they have in common. My relationship with Tracy started like a too-good-to-be-true fairy tale as well. I can never be certain.

Because I'm thinking all of this while Tess's fingers meander down and her lips stay fastened on my nipple, my body hardly responds when her finger circles around my clit. Yet, I don't stop her. I want this. Not just for me, but for her as well. Tess is not Tracy, I repeat to myself, Tess is not Tracy.

She must find wetness when her finger trails along my lips, because she easily slips in, which just goes to show that what the body does isn't always aligned with what the mind is think-ing, but I know from the first split second she's inside of me that it will be a lost cause. I'm in my head too much and as much as I want to—so desperately—let go, I know I ruined it before she even started.

"Tess." I bring a hand to her hair, stroke her, while my other hand finds hers and I stop her motion. "Please."

She retreats instantly and looks up. "What is it?" Nothing but worry in her glance. "Did I do something wrong?"

"No, absolutely not." I curl my fingers around her wrist, not wanting to let go of it ever again. I feel foolish and stupid for ruining a beautiful moment. "It's not you, it's me."

"Tell me." She shuffles upward until our gazes are aligned. "Talk to me, Laura. I want to know what you're thinking."

Tell me what you're thinking. One of Tracy's classic lines when she was in full-on restitution mode. "I'm sorry, I just—it has just been a bit much."

"It's fine," Tess says, her hand lingering just above my breasts. "I understand."

Do you? I want to ask. *How can you possibly understand?* But this is not Tess's fault. Maybe I'm just not ready for the light of the day to shine upon me when we do this.

I shake my head, not as an expression of dismissiveness, but because I want to shake the self-pity off me. The one thing I've always tried very hard not to wallow in. Yes, bad things happened to me, and marrying Tracy was an awful decision in hindsight, but I didn't know. If there were ever any clues as to the person she really was, I can't hold it against myself any longer for not spotting them. I'm not psychic. I can't read people's innermost thoughts. I'm just a regular woman. I was a victim, but I'm not anymore.

"Why don't we take a shower?" I trail my finger through Tess's hair. "You and me together."

"Okay." Tess nods solemnly. "But, Laura, please know that you can talk to me about anything."

"I know. I do know that." Here I go again. If there's one thing that annoys me most about myself it's this line that I keep repeating endlessly. "I will when I'm ready."

"And another thing." A smile breaks through the grave expression on her face. "You'd better get used to me because I'm not going anywhere."

32

TESS

"Are you ready for this?" I ask Laura. Although she has come to dinner at the Douglas house a dozen times by now, this time is different. This time we're together. A fact I wasn't able to hide from Mom and Dad for one second when I came home after spending the night at Laura's.

"Of course I am." Laura looks more scrumptious than ever, despite her wearing the same kind of white t-shirt she always wears. How would she react if I bought her a blue one as a present, or a red one? Her hair has grown back to the same length as when we first met. And every time she pulls back from me—every time the past catches up with her—I remember how she was when we first met. Her body language all defensive, her words not much more inviting. When she retreats in on herself and goes all silent, I hope she doesn't blame herself for holding back on me, because, every day, I am witness to how much she has changed already.

Moby sniffs her shoes and jeans, probably smelling Socks on them.

"We should go inside," Laura says, leaning into me a little.

"I know." I cup her cheeks in my hands. As soon as we go

inside I won't have her to myself anymore. There is so much still left to discover, so much left to learn. "Dad made a cake."

Mom hugs Laura like she is a long lost daughter returning home. "We were so happy when Tess told us," she says. I probably didn't warn Laura enough about this, about how they can be. I should have known that their single daughter finding love would send them into overdrive. I've learned how to rein in my Douglas enthusiasm a little around Laura when the circumstances call for it, but my parents don't know about Laura's secret and Mom is extra switched on today.

Laura smiles at her but then I have to look away because Dad thrusts me in the biceps with his elbow. I glance at him but he doesn't say anything, just stands there giving me a thumbs-up with a big grin on his face. If I weren't raised in this family, I'd surely be rolling my eyes at him but, unlike Laura, I've been blessed with the most supportive family that ever lived. And always, as has become a habit over the past few weeks, I can't help but wonder what Laura's thinking. Is it too late for her to experience the warmth of unconditional parental support the way I have? Does being here with my Mom and Dad remind her of her parents and how awfully they've treated her?

"Sorry we're late." Megan and Toby barge in. "Emma and Max both have colds and Scott seems to be coming down with one as well."

Toby, just on the cusp, I think, of being too old to let us all kiss him, makes the rounds. I kiss him hard on the forehead.

"I'll make chicken soup," Mom immediately says. "It will cure them in no time."

"Thanks for feeding us, Mommy." Megan kisses Mom on the cheek. "You're a lifesaver."

Once we've all sat down to dinner and drinks have been poured and plates filled, Dad raises his glass and says, "To Laura."

Though I think it's a little over the top to be proposing a toast at this stage, I sit there beaming with pride nonetheless.

Toby, his glass of water half-raised, asks, "Why are we holding up our glasses for Laura?"

"Because Auntie Tess and Laura are a couple now," Megan says. "You know, like Dad and me."

"Okay," Toby says, looking confused for a few seconds, then turns to me. "Are you getting married?"

I giggle nervously. "It's a bit too early for that," I say.

"Why? Mom and Dad are married. And then they had me." Christ, the boy is just like his mother—and me. He doesn't know when to stop.

"All in good time, Toby," Laura says. "People don't just meet and get married straight away."

"But you've known each other for aaaages." He stresses the first part of the word with the seriousness only a child can muster.

"Toby, that's enough questions from you," Megan butts in. "You'll be the first to know when Auntie Tess and Laura get married, okay?" She shoots me an apologetic smile. "Now eat your vegetables."

Later, when Megan and I are filling the dishwasher while Mom and Dad have taken Laura and Toby outside to show them the inflatable swimming pool they've installed for the summer, Megan says, "You look happy, sis. You have that glow about you."

I wish I could confide in my sister about this. I wish I could share with her—the person I've always shared everything with, from the smallest to the biggest things that happened in my life —what Laura's burden is, but I know I need to keep my big mouth shut. I know if I don't I'll lose Laura's trust forever, and I've only just gained a fraction of it.

"I'm happy. It's still early days, though the family is treating it more like an engagement already."

"We've just... you know, been waiting," Megan says.

"Well, I've been waiting too, Megs. I've been waiting for a long time." Memories of our first night together pop up in my brain. The relief I felt, the sheer joy of being with another woman again. And the right one at that. If I'd somehow managed to crawl into bed with Sherry the cowgirl, it might have been satisfying for two minutes, but it would have been nothing compared to the all-obliterating bliss I felt with Laura.

"I know you have." Megan stops piling dishes for a second and I feel her gaze burning on the back of my head. "At times it felt as though you'd wait forever. It made me wonder what you were so afraid of."

"What do you mean?" I raise to my full height and look Megan straight in the eyes.

"You could have made more effort to find someone, perhaps?"

What is Megan getting at? "This is Nelson, Texas, Megs. Eligible lesbian bachelorettes don't exactly grown on trees here."

"Well, duh. But I sometimes asked myself if you weren't using us, the family, as an excuse not to put yourself out there."

"What? No." That's the second time in a very short period of time I'm being questioned about this—and by my own sister no less, the person I always wanted to stay for the most. "Not everyone is as lucky as you, that's all. You met Scott in college and he moved to Nelson for you."

"Yes, he did, but that's just the thing though. If he hadn't wanted to move here, I would have followed him. If he'd wanted to settle in Houston or Dallas or even out of state, I'm pretty sure I wouldn't have stuck around here, moping for the love I lost."

"You can't compare the two situations. When you met Scott, you *knew*. I've fallen in love, sure, but never to the extent that I was willing to sacrifice proximity to my family. Remember Houston? I did try, you know."

"Of course I remember you living in Houston. I knew that woman wasn't right for you from the get-go, by the way, and I distinctly remember telling you that, but you ignored my twin-sister intuition. You ignored The Force, Tessie." Megan has a grin on her face now. We can never keep it too serious between us for too long a time.

"Then do tell me what you think about Laura. What does The Force have to say about her?" I look at her closely, lest I miss any signs of disapproval on her face.

"Laura is great. I don't know her that well just yet, but all I need to do is look at you when you're with her and I just know she's right for you." Megan pauses. "But, I don't know, there's something about her I can't put my finger on. Perhaps the very thing that makes her so attractive to you. I look at her and I see someone who's the opposite of you. Not just in the way she dresses or how she always comes across so serious, but her personality is the opposite of bubbly."

"She has been through a lot, Megs." It's out of my mouth before I even think about a suitable reply.

"So you keep saying." This time, it's Megan's turn to examine my face for signs of something I'm not telling her— me, her sister who tells her everything. "Is this about her parents? I can still see them arrive at Milly's funeral. Such disrespect." Megan shakes her head.

"They certainly didn't help." Again, that war waging within me. I know for a fact that Megan would keep whatever secret I told her. "Mom and Dad are a million times more Christian than they are and they never even go to church anymore." Deflect, I tell myself. It's a good strategy.

"The way they sat so stiffly on those chairs at Laura's house at the reception, keeping away from everyone, as though we were all Satan's spawn." Megan seems to have taken the bait.

"Can you understand now why I could never leave this family? You make every other family out there look bad." I try to drive my point home—something Megs and I both like to do with each other—and make a joke in the process. And I know I don't have an ounce of darkness within me and, perhaps, that's why Laura is drawn to *me*. I'm her light at the end of the tunnel.

The kitchen door opens and Dad walks in. "Tessie, darlin', I've convinced Laura to try that craft brandy I've had for years. The one neither one of you, nor that husband of yours, Megs, wants to touch." He seems mightily pleased with himself.

Mom, Toby, and Laura file into the kitchen. "What have you girls been doing?" Mom asks. "I thought my kitchen would be spic-and-span by now." She turns to Laura. "Put those two together and they get absolutely nothing done. Always gossiping and giggling and forgetting the task at hand." She comes over and gives me a kiss on the cheek. "Why don't you join Dad and Laura in the lounge, I'll take it from here."

My gaze finds Laura's and the wink she shoots me fills me with an unspeakable burst of happiness.

***

"THIS IS SO UNCOMFORTABLE." I huddle next to Laura under the duvet. "You'd better not touch me inappropriately."

"I can't believe this room." Laura slurs her words. "It looks like you never changed it since you were a teenager."

"Tomorrow, when your brandy goggles are off, you can have another look at it and apologize for what you just said." I perch on one elbow and look at Laura. "What were you thinking, babe? You barely drink and then you let Dad liquor you up like that?"

"I could tell it would mean a lot to him." Laura folds her

fingers behind her head and looks at me with the most relaxed expression I've seen on her face.

"You don't need to impress him, Laura. We all love you already."

"Oh really?" Apparently, she's not too far gone to defy me. "Earl loves me?"

"He's fond of you. I'm sure of that."

"Because I took his daughter off the streets." She giggles so hard she snorts.

"I think you should close your eyes now and go to sleep." There's no point in prolonging this conversation, although it's a joy to see Laura this giddy and uninhibited.

"I don't want to sleep, Tess." Under the sheets, her hand clamps down on my thigh.

"Is that right?" No matter how drunk Laura is, her touch shoots through me like an electric shock. Every time. "And what would you do instead?"

"Maybe something you've never done in this room." Her hand travels higher, her voice is deep and alcohol-soaked.

"Laura, sweetie, your hand might be close to the money, but I don't think it has enough energy left to do anything of the sort. And my parents are a little too close for my comfort." I cover her hand in mine.

"Your family is just so… nice. How is it even possible?" Her words are coming slower now. "I thought families like yours only existed in the most unrealistic fiction, in children's books or something."

"No father would get his daughter's brand new girlfriend drunk on brandy in any children's book," I retort. I should turn off the light but I'm enjoying looking at Laura in her current state too much.

"No women ever had girlfriends in the books I read as a child," Laura says. Her hand starts squirming underneath mine, pulling itself free and riding up a little higher. It stops right below the hem of my panties. "But, foolishly, as a child, I did believe my family was perfect. Until I found out they weren't. The first big disillusionment of my life."

"Nobody is—" I start saying, but Laura just keeps on talking.

"The second one was Tracy, of course. At first, I thought she was perfect as well. Maybe because I wanted her to be, though I should have known. After all, I had first hand experience with perfect people falling from grace. But I didn't see. I didn't know. For the longest time I wondered what exactly saying 'I do' to me did to her. The very first time she hit me, I was stunned more than hurt. I was shocked. You hardly feel pain when you're in shock, I guess. I don't know." She falls silent after that.

Instinctively, I inch closer toward her, throw an arm over her chest.

"I need you, Tess," she whispers with a sob in her voice. "Only someone like you will do for me. Someone as honest and utterly nice like you. I promise you I will always be honest with you and the thing about you is that you don't even need to make that promise to me, because I already know you will be. I see your decency and I know it's not a front. I just know that."

My eyes fill with tears. Maybe this is not the right time, but I'm saying it anyway. "I love you, Laura. With everything I have."

"I love you too." Her voice is barely audible, but I understood.

I HARDLY SLEEP for several reasons, but the main one is Laura's words echoing in my mind throughout the night. That, and she snored so loudly it sounded like someone was about to hack up my bed with a chainsaw.

It's just gone past 5 a.m. and, for the umpteenth time, I give her a gentle push to, I hope, coax her onto her side without waking her.

"Hm," she moans. "What?" Her eyes fly open with what looks like sheer terror.

"It's all right. You're at the Douglas ranch." She must have had a nightmare.

"Keep me awake," she whispers. "I don't want to fall back asleep."

I nod, shuffling closer to her. "Bad dream, snore bear?"

She shakes her head. "I don't really remember. I just remember being irrationally afraid of something."

"Was it a bear, perhaps?" I smile.

"A bear? I don't know. Why?" Her eyes are sleep-crusted and her voice is hoarse and raw.

"It's what kept *me* awake." I run a finger over her cheek and wait until her brain starts working properly.

"Did I snore?" Disproportionate panic crosses her face. "Shit."

"It's fine, Laura. You drank too much. It happens." I kiss her quickly on the cheek. "I'll survive."

She shakes her head. "I woke up once with Tracy's hands wrapped around my neck. When I opened my eyes, she said, 'if you don't stop making those godawful noises, I swear to God, I'll choke you to death.' And I believed every word she said."

"Jesus Christ, Laura." As much as Laura's revelation feels like a punch to the gut—and as much as it would make *me* want to kill Tracy if she weren't already dead—I'm also glad that Laura is opening up more, that she's willing to show me this side of her, this look deep inside her wounded soul. "I'm so sorry." My words feel wholly inadequate but there's really nothing else to say. Not even I, bright and fun-spirited Tess Douglas, can reason this sort of evil away with a quip.

"But... I'm moving on, Tess," Laura says while she turns on her side. "With you." She draws her lips into a small smile. Her skin looks a bit ashen and the wrinkles around her eyes seem to have deepened overnight. "And I may have a hell of a hangover today, but I remember every word I said to you last night."

"I love you," I say again. "Now you should probably go back to sleep."

"What if the bear returns?" There's laughter in Laura's eyes now.

"I'll pretend it's a teddy bear and cuddle it profusely," I joke, waiting.

"I love you too." Her eyes have gone serious again. "And I'm not going anywhere either."

LAURA

"Where are you taking me?" Tess asks. I picked her up at *The Ledger's* office just when I thought the light outside was beginning to look perfect. That thin strip of time between late afternoon and early evening when it changes into something out of this world, takes on a glow of purples and oranges you can only find in nature.

"You'll see." I drive us in my old Honda to Tess's land. It's not far and Tess is a smart girl. She's just playing dumb to amuse us.

"Laura Baker, full of mysteries." She puts her hand on my knee and squeezes tightly.

"We've arrived." I park my car where Tess parked hers when she took me here first. I couldn't tell her at the time, let alone admit it to myself, but it was the first time I could possibly conceive of Tess and me as a 'thing'. It was impossible not to recognize the sparks flying between us, the chemistry that coated our words and, perhaps, shaped how we sat and looked at each other. We were becoming fast friends and, underneath the platonic falling in love that happens when you make a new friend like that, something else was stirring. That's why I wanted to bring her back here. This place means something to me now, and not a lot of places in Nelson do, because I don't have much history in this town yet.

"Well, what a surprise," Tess says, her voice dripping with irony. "I would never have guessed." She turns to me, her eyes shiny with glee. "It's the pull of the land, Laura, I get it."

If she keeps this up, I'll never be able to make my heartfelt request. But Tess knows when to shut up, despite her big mouth and the words that just keep rolling from it. She knows when a moment calls for silence, which makes her even more perfect for me.

I have questioned Tess's perfection, because how can any person be so good at so many things? How can she be so patient and so understanding and so pretty at the same time? It seems like an impossible combination. Because Tracy was these things too when we first met. She picked up the broken pieces of my daughter-heart long after I had cut off contact with my parents. She restored my faith in humanity, and she was a looker as well. Until she destroyed my heart all over again.

But what I see now, is the difference between them. Every day, I see where Tess comes from. I know the people who made her into the person she is and, every time, I think, how can she not be the amazing woman that she is? And I stop questioning her perfection because she's not perfect—no one is—but what she is, is perfect for me. She's the light to my darkness. The voice to my stillness. The smile to my sad face.

"Give me a hand, will you?" I hand Tess the blanket I brought. It's hot and humid outside and sweat already pools in the small of my back. I'm wearing a t-shirt that Tess gave me a week ago, saying, "I think it's time the color of your t-shirts started reflecting the color I've brought into your life." Only Tess can say things like that without making them sound silly —can make me believe something like that. She handed me a turquoise v-neck and said it would bring out the color of my eyes.

Once we've sat down and I've handed her a bottle of beer from the cooler I brought, I say, "I did some research and building a house here is not inconceivable."

Tess looks at me from under her lashes. If she's surprised at all by what I just said, she doesn't show it. "Research, huh?"

"Just looking to the future." I look at her, because, especially in this light, and on this evening, I can't keep my eyes off her. To her left, the sun is sinking deeper, but still blasting Texas heat. It's June now and Chicago will be warming up, getting ready for its own hot and humid summer. I look at her because she is my future.

"I always knew bringing you here had impressed you," Tess says.

What I've learned is that, unless I reveal something nasty about my past that snaps her right out of whatever's going on in her head, it's not possible to cut right to the chase with Tess. She always has a deflection ready, a quip to steer the conversation any way she'd like it to go.

"What I'm trying to say"—I've also learned to, when I really want to make a point, ignore Tess's defense mechanisms—"is that I can see us living here someday."

She's silent for a few seconds, then says, "Are you going to build us a house, Laura?" That smirk she's sporting slowly develops into a smile.

"I'm not sure my DIY skills stretch that far." I inch a little closer and take her hand in mine. "I can't do what you've done for me, Tess. I can't even take you to meet my parents, show you where I come from. Maybe one day we'll go to Chicago and I'll show you the place where I was happy once, but it would be a mere act of looking back. I know I need to look forward now. Moving to Nelson was the first step I took. I hadn't even thought it through properly. I just needed to get away and came here because of Aunt Milly, and then I met you. And you started pestering me, and charming me, and getting under my skin. And look at us now? I'm not the same woman who left Chicago, and that's all down to you."

"What can I say?" Tess winds her fingers tightly around mine. "Meeting a dark, handsome stranger with brooding, mysterious blue eyes brings out the pestering side of me." She lifts up my hand and plants a kiss on it. "You may not realize it, but you've done plenty for me too."

"There is one more thing you can do for me." I take control of our joined hands and bring them to my lips. I kiss the tip of her index finger, then take it into my mouth.

From the way she cocks her head, I can tell that Tess is catching my drift. The sun is low now, but still strong enough to illuminate the activity I'm referring to in a way that would please me. "What would that be?" Tess gets that smoldering look in her eyes—a look I haven't always been able to reciprocate.

"I want you to make me come on your land." It sounds quite ridiculous when I say it like that—not that it sounded more dignified in my head when I hatched my plan. "I want to make love to you here, outside, in the last of the light, and I want you to look me straight in the eyes when you do." It's my way of saying that I want to surrender to her completely, that I want to expel the cobwebs from my brain—those memories of what I've done and what was done to me that tend to pop up at the most inconvenient times.

"Okay." Tess nods solemnly. Her defenses are all down now. My honesty has that effect on her. "I will happily oblige." She scooches a little closer, the hem of her dress riding up in the process, giving me a nice view of her thigh. "I'm cool that way." She leans in to kiss me. It's not a gentle kiss, but one with purpose and determination. "You really are full of surprises," she says when we break apart and she pushes me down onto the blanket. She gazes down at me. "What if someone comes along?"

I shake my head. "I scouted the place at this time of the day on various occasions. No one comes here."

Tess chuckles, her lips curving into a grin. "Of course, you have." She gives a knowing smile. "But you'll see, the universe is crazy that way, today of all days, someone will drive past."

"The prospect of that will only make me come so much harder," I whisper. This calls Tess back to the task at hand. She bites her bottom lip, nods again, and leans in.

Tess folds her long body over mine, curls her hands around my neck and kisses me until, when I open my eyes again, the sun has sunk dangerously low. "I want it to be light," I whisper as soon as I get the chance.

Tess understands and proceeds to hoist up my t-shirt, exposing my bare chest. "No bra, huh?" She narrows her eyes. "I hope you know it's a sign of how respectful I am toward you that I didn't even notice." She doesn't wait for a response—and I'm sure she did notice, but just didn't say anything about it— and goes straight for a nipple, sucking it hard between her lips.

My bare chest exposed to the air like that feels like the entirety of nature connecting with my body. Tracy would never have been up for this. She was way too controlling for that. Which is why I picked this spot, why I wanted some out-door loving. *Stop it*, a voice in my head scolds me, because this is what I do and once my thoughts start spiraling down, there really is no return. I brought Tess to this spot to ban Tracy from my mind and, if only for the next fifteen minutes, the ghost of Tracy Hunt will leave me in peace. It's the only way I can move forward, remove myself from my past—*and* the only way for me to enjoy this.

Tess pushes my breasts together and looks at them as though they are the singular biggest feast ever offered to her in her life. By the way her breath is coming faster, and her fingers start kneading more profoundly, I can tell she's beginning to lose herself. That she doesn't care that we are doing this out in the open, free from the privacy and, more importantly for me, the oppressing constraints of a house, a room, a bed. On this field, in this light—dimming, but still there—is the only place where I can feel completely free.

Rachel always used to say, after one of her conquests ended in a one-night stand, "When you know, you know, and I know she's not the one." In this very moment, I know Tess is the one. I can't even rationally explain it, which is an even bigger leap for me than taking a chance at dating her, but I just know. As her lips reach the waistband of my jeans, and she plants kiss after kiss on the sensitive skin there, and I can't even see her face, all I see is her. Her smile and the kindness it radiates. How her eyes light up every time she looks at me.

Tess unsnaps my jeans, lowers the zipper, and starts tugging them down. I'm not sure me kicking my legs about in an excited fashion is helping, but I'm eager—oh so eager—for what's to come, and I don't want to miss my moment. I don't want this evening to fail me.

Once my jeans and underwear are off me, I spread my legs wide. And, oh, the sensation of the hot Texas breeze on my nether lips, of being exposed to nature, of doing this under a slowly darkening sky, is more than enough to flood my clit with pulsing desire.

Tess climbs up until her face is level with mine, her knee pressing between my legs. She doesn't say anything, just looks at me as though she effortlessly understands why I need this. She kisses me long and deep, while her hand follows the path her lips traced earlier. It halts at a nipple to pinch it into a hard peak, before slowly meandering down over the expanse of gooseflesh my skin has become, until her finger hovers over my clit. Though I can't feel it, it's as if I can sense the promise in its proximity there. We break from our passionate lip-lock and she gazes into my eyes. It's not easy to just glance back at her without qualms, to make like I'm very self-assured about this. But what Tess has done so swiftly, so easily, is peel away a thick layer of fear I was carrying around with me. She scratched it away to reveal a little more of my true self to her with every day that has passed. And that's why I can now, finally, give myself up to her, here, on her land, where, I hope, one day we'll live together.

Tess's finger slips and slides along my wet, wet lips. Her mouth twitches in a display of focus and her eyes narrow as she pushes inside of me. And as she does, I know I'm home. Not because of the land, or because I've grown to love life in Nelson, but because of the person who is inside of me—in every cell of me.

I look up into those gray-green eyes as she pushes deeper, harder, inserts another finger, and I let go. I let go of everything that has held me back up until this point in my life. It's just me and Tess under the fading evening light. And I don't close my eyes when I feel the first heat swarm underneath my skin. I keep my eyes on her, the real woman of my dreams.

Tess adds her thumb to the action and she lets it press against my clit every time she strokes me deep inside and this level of intimacy is not something I dreamed I'd ever be capable of again, but here I am, surrendering to Tess, reaching those new heights easily now, because it's with the right woman.

She intensifies the pace, thrusts deep within me, flicks more determinedly with her thumb. I can feel her breath on my face, short gusts passing along my lips, mixing with moans that come from my own mouth, piercing the Texas air.

Then it takes me. Everything she's doing to me and everything I feel for her crashes over me in a wave of tingling, limb-stiffening warmth. I try not to close my eyes, to stay with her in this moment, because it deepens the sensation in my flesh, reaches deeper into my core.

When I collapse underneath her, my limbs soft, my skin covered in a sheen of sweat, my entire being is so relaxed I couldn't even stop the tears welling in my eyes if I wanted to. But I don't want to. I can cry in front of Tess now. I can do everything in front of her now.

TESS

I've convinced Laura to share babysitting duties with me, and after all three children have finally gone to bed—each more reluctant than the last because of the excitement of having a new person in the house—we sit on Scott and Megan's back porch with a chilled glass of chardonnay. Laura isn't so afraid of consuming alcohol anymore, though I hardly think she'll be touching Dad's brandy anytime soon.

"Your sister must have been thrilled when you moved back to Nelson," Laura says. "All this free babysitting that you do."

"I don't mind and, besides, silly as it may sound, it gives me some much-needed privacy. I can just flick through some channels, or walk around in my underwear, or bring a girl over." I catch Laura's gaze.

"No hanky-panky tonight, babe." She grins.

"But to answer your question, yes, I think Megan was very thrilled when I came back. Not just for the babysitting, though there is that."

"Does she ever… do anything for you in return?" Laura asks.

I quirk up my eyebrows, unsure what to reply to that. The

question has never even entered my mind. "She gave birth to three little people who adore the hell out of me. Children I love dearly, but I don't have to parent, only spoil rotten. That's a pretty good trade-off. Plus, I get to keep my ultra-toned body."

"See what you did there?" Laura asks. "You diverted my attention from the matter at hand by mentioning your ultra-toned body." Her grin has grown seductive.

We both know my body is far from toned, but I'll happily play along. "What I can't get off *my* mind," I say, "is *your* ultra-toned body naked on *my* land." Unlike me, Laura is super fit, though her running routine has suffered greatly since we went on our first official date. We do, however, engage in plenty of other calorie-burning activities.

"What can I say, babe? The thought of you owning all that sprawling Texas land made me horny as hell." Laura chuckles.

"I can see it too, you know. You and me in our brand-new house. Socks frolicking on the lawn. We can try to take Moby, though I doubt Mom will let me. But we can adopt another dog. The kids visiting their awesome aunts." I take a quick sip from my wine. "Though what we are doing right now is extremely lesbian. We're skipping the U-haul altogether and starting to talk about building a house together straightaway."

Laura purses her lips together. "We can always practice at my house." She drums her fingers onto the table. "We can start with a drawer," she muses. "Well, actually, I have so few clothes and belongings, you may as well have most of the wardrobe and the other closet space."

"Are you asking me what I think you're asking me?" My palms break out into a sweat.

"I'm asking you what you're *hearing* me ask you, babe." Laura plants her elbows on the table and looks at me intently. "You're at my house all the time, anyway. We might as well make it official and stop fussing around with leaving the keys under the mat and texting back and forth about where and when we'll meet." She shoots me a kind grin. "That is, of course, if you are ready to move out of your parents' house. I know you're not really old enough yet."

"Funny," I bite back playfully. "But handy. And we won't even need to rent that U-Haul. We can use Dad's truck to move my meager belongings."

"You can walk around in your underwear as much as you like. Or without." Under the table, Laura's toe sneaks up my shin.

"Or in one of your t-shirts, which barely cover me, anyway."

"While we dream of our house," Laura says, her voice serious again.

"I would love that, Laura." I could grab her hand over the table, or clasp her feet in between mine underneath it, but it's not enough. I need more. I push myself away from the table and walk to her. I put my hands on her shoulders and kiss her for a long time.

"This was a bit of a spur-of-the-moment decision. One I've been thinking about, but, well, I don't exactly have a spare key on me to make it official," Laura says.

"Give it to me when we get home." I peck her on the forehead. I must have driven past Milly's house a million times in my lifetime, but never would I have guessed I'd one day end up living there with another woman. With the woman I love.

WE'VE FINISHED THE BOTTLE, me drinking two-thirds in my giddy enthusiasm and Laura one and a half slowly-sipped glasses, when she asks me, her eyes on me, her voice low, "When did you get your heart broken for the first time?"

"It must be after ten if you're coming out with the hard questions," I joke.

Laura looks at me. "Why is it a hard question?"

I push out my bottom lip. "I don't know. Because I don't think about things like that, I guess. I'm shallow that way."

"You're anything but shallow, Tess. I'm just curious and I'd like to know who in their right mind ever had the audacity to dump you."

"Okay." I lean back in my chair, thinking. I'm not really one to dwell on past heartbreaks, but there is one instance of it that I've always carried with me as a reminder of how things should never turn out again. "Her name was Chelsea. She was in my English Lit class in my first year at college. She came from this big family in Florida and, especially next to me, she was tiny. But full of life, you know? A real spitfire. I fell in love with her. Like really properly in love. But, as you would have it, she was straight. Which didn't stop me falling for her harder every day, no, every hour we spent together. We hung out a lot, studied together... I watched her drunkenly make out with way too many guys at parties, until one night we just ended up in bed together. It just happened. One of those college things, I guess. But of course my immature, vulnerable heart didn't see it that way." I pause, look at my empty glass, decide against opening another bottle of wine because I like the way Laura is looking at me right now. She might well be the world's greatest listener. Her head is tilted, her eyes focused on me, but not staring too hard.

"I fell deeper in love, of course, and we embarked on this sort of half-baked relationship. We kept it to ourselves, though I did tell Megan, of course. Who, she would have me state for the record I'm sure, told me I was out of my mind falling for a girl like that. Of course, I wouldn't have any of that. Megan didn't know what she was talking about. She didn't know what it was like to be me blah, blah, blah. You know how it goes at that age. I was smitten, well and truly head-over-heels in love. And it was amazing for about five minutes. We had some amazing sex, though I may be remembering that wrong and might have painted it in a better light than it was over the years. Anyway, she was really sweet to me behind closed doors, to the extent that I actually believed it could work between us if I gave her some time. Because this was all new to her, she had to get used to it, she'd never been with a girl before." I exhale deeply. "I imagine you can guess the rest."

"Tell me," Laura urges, in a voice so soft and gentle, just the sound of it can undo all the wrongs I've experienced throughout my entire life.

"She met a guy. A stupid beefcake wrestler from Denver. Ears like this." I cup my hands behind my ears and make them stick out. "Abs for days. Three times the size of her. I have no clue what she ever saw in him, but, well, she dumped me for him. Oldest story in the book. A lesbian college affair gone wrong. It might have made me a big fat cliché, but gosh dang it, it hurt like hell. I saw them everywhere, of course. Every single day was a reminder of how I wasn't with her anymore. It was pretty awful for a while. Don't tell Megan she was right, by the way."

"Don't tell Megan she was right about what?" Out of nowhere, Megan appears behind us. I was so wrapped up in my story that I didn't hear them come home.

"Nothing," I say quickly, but she's my sister, and, automatically, I share, anyway. "I was just telling Laura about Chelsea Watts, my college crush."

"Ah, stating very clearly I was right about that whole shebang, I hope?" Megan asks.

"The kids go down well?" Scott asks with his usual matter-of-fact-ness, ignoring his wife.

"Fine," Laura says. "Good as gold." It's a blatant lie, the way they were fussing and trying to manipulate us into letting them stay up past their bed time.

"Guess what!" Now that my sister is here, I need to share

the next bit of information as well. "Laura asked me to move in with her."

Megan looks from me to Laura, then punches the air as though she has just won a big prize. "That's awesome news."

"You're just saying that 'cause now the kids can each have a room at Earl and Maura's," Scott says. "Whereas I, your beloved brother-in-law, am genuinely happy for you." Awkwardly, he pats Laura on the shoulder. "Congratulations," he says.

"We'd better drink to that," Megan says, and holds up the empty bottle of wine.

"You know that it's very unethical to pay babysitters in wine, don't you, honey?" Scott says, then goes inside to fetch another bottle.

LAURA

ONE YEAR LATER

Tracy's parents were Catholic, but an altogether different kind of religious than my own. They didn't raise her in the church, nor did they break all ties with her when she came out. They proudly attended our wedding ceremony and didn't have a kind word to say about my parents' absence. When the time came for Tracy to be buried—a process I was not very involved in—they opted for a Catholic ceremony and cemetery.

Arriving at the graveyard now, the religious symbolism jars me only for an instant, but it doesn't bother me. I had to give up my hatred for the religion that banned me from my parents' lives a long time ago, before I let it consume me. But, walking along the gravestones adorned with crosses and words of how great the buried were, does make me balk at the hypocrisy of it all. As though death makes everything right.

It's the first time I've set foot here and Tess is holding on tightly to my arm. After Tracy died, I was such a wreck, such a shadow of a woman, I didn't have it in me to come here. First, I thought I had no right after giving her that final push—the very last time someone touched her when she was alive. Then, after the anger had set in, I didn't want to visit anymore. Not long after, I left for Texas. But I know I need to do this now. I didn't come to Chicago for this purpose alone, but I discussed it with Tess, and it's an integral part of our trip. Though I never had the guts to stand up to Tracy when she was alive, I can still do so now. It won't change anything. What happened will still have happened. Her parents will still hate me for the rest of their lives. Our friends, the ones who didn't know, will never fully understand what went down that night. But to me, it *will* make a difference. I've come here to put the past behind me.

When we arrive at the spot where her remains are buried, at first, I don't feel anything. It's as though that veneer of cold hard steel has wrapped itself around my heart again, shutting everything out. The sun is high in a blue sky. The grass is so green. It's a beautiful day, and Tess and I could be tourists visiting the graves of the handful of famous people buried here. But we're not. We're here for Tracy Hunt. My deceased wife. The woman whose life I took, but who robbed me of life long before that.

Tess doesn't say anything, just leans into me a little closer. I left Chicago over a year ago and have told Tess everything I remember. From the very first time I met Tracy, with her asymmetrical bangs, loud gestures but soft voice, to the last time I saw her, her skull cracked and blood pooling around her dead body. And I have cried. I have cried all the tears that wouldn't come since Tracy died. Her death still haunts me—I will never forget the instant, the shocking silence of it, the immediate knowledge that something terrible, something irrevocable has happened. When you take a life, no matter the circumstances, your own life changes. But the difference is that, no matter how different it is now—and thank goodness for that—my life does go on. I'm alive. I'm still breathing. And I have Tess.

"Do you know that Al Capone used to be buried here?" I say, just to say something, to fill the silence hanging over us. "Not anymore, though."

"She was a criminal too, Laura," Tess says. "She committed crimes against you."

But I never filed one single police report, I think. I know better than to say it out loud. Heck, I even know better than to still think this way. I never breathed a word about their daughter's true nature to her parents. As far as I know, they'll go to their own grave believing it was a stupid accident, one of those inexplicable twists of fate that life can throw at you. I felt insurmountable guilt for my parents-in-law's grief for the longest time, because to have to bury a child is not something you can recover from either. But Tracy *was* their child, without them she wouldn't have existed, and if they ever knew about her uncontrollable temper, they never let on.

"She was many things," I whisper, while I feel that cold fist around my heart unclenching slowly. "I lost respect for her long before she died and I think that was the hardest. Bruises heal, but to live with that toxic mixture of utter disdain and constant fear. It didn't make any sense. It was like being two people. She was two people, but so was I. I was never a pushover before her. I didn't let my parents walk over me when they wanted to change me, I just left. But maybe I used up all my leaving power by doing that. And every time something happened, I vowed I would leave her. I would pack my bags the very next night, the next hour, but I never did. Because then Tracy became *her* other person again, that person I had fallen in love with, and through some strange, defensive trick of the mind, I did respect her again. I respected her remorse. I respected what we had between us, the love that didn't seem to languish. Being in an abusive relationship is just one endless mind game. In the end, she did manage to change me into someone I wasn't. Or I was deep-down all along. I don't know."

"I know who you are, Laura." This is what Tess is so good at. She takes my claims about myself, my guilt and the disdain I have for my personality when I was with Tracy, and tosses them out the window by replacing them with words like this. "You are brave and strong and beautiful and kind-hearted. That's who you are."

"That's who I am with you." I turn to face her and kiss her in front of Tracy's grave, while realizing that this was the reason I needed to come here. To be able to do this. The ultimate act of looking at the future, and no longer be ruled by my past.

TESS

FOUR YEARS LATER

"If I had known in advance you could hear the roar of the crowd from here, I would never have moved here," Laura says the exact same thing she says every Friday night the Cougars have a home game.

"You can hear it all throughout Nelson, babe." I have my same-old reply at the ready. "Rub my feet?" I bring my left foot to her lap.

"Can't you see my lap is taken?" She rubs the back of Socks's head, who instantly pushes himself against her hand. That cat was an attention whore from the very beginning. The biggest difference between when Laura just brought him home to her Aunt Milly's house back in the day and now, is that now he's a lazy fat ginger and no longer that spritely kitten with the high-pitched meow who slept on Laura's pillow.

"Can't *you* see I'm carrying our offspring?" Ostentatiously, I pat my giant belly.

"How much longer until I have a cousin to play with?" Emma asks. She's sitting with us on the back porch of our newly-built house, instead of attending the Cougars game, and pissing off her father greatly in the process.

"Three more weeks," I say.

"I'll rub your feet, Auntie Tess." She has the sweetest smile on her face.

"That's very nice of you, Emma, but rubbing pregnant spouses' feet is not a niece's job. Why don't you go pry Socks from Auntie Laura's lap, so I can put my feet there."

Emma jumps up. Chunkie, our chocolate labrador, follows on her heel—that dog would follow her to school after she has spent the night at ours. In her rough and careless seven-year-old manner, she liberates Socks from Laura's lap. Socks is good-natured enough to be toyed with like that, but Chunkie gives a jealous little bark.

"Daddy said that if Socks has babies we can have one," Emma states proudly.

Laura and I both burst out into a giggle. Scott can be so cruel sometimes—funny, but cruel to his daughter.

"Emma, darling," Laura begins. "Socks is a male cat. He's not going to have babies."

"But you and Auntie Tess are two ladies and you're having a baby," she says matter-of-factly.

I wonder what else my brother-in-law has told her. I'm too exhausted by being with child to explain my pregnancy to Emma. She's too young to understand it, anyway.

"Maybe Chunkie and Socks can have a baby as well," she adds, not giving up hope just yet.

"That would be a really cute animal," Laura jumps in. She has finally started rubbing my feet and it feels so good I could do with some peace and quiet right about now. I've started respecting my sister much more for going through this three times in her life.

I close my eyes and block out Laura and Emma's chatter, and think about the child we're about to have. The new life we've created. I'm almost forty-three. Once Laura and I concluded that we both wanted a child, we had to act immediately. We didn't have the luxury of time to analyze every emotion, worry or doubt. We just had to go for it and do it. We set the process in motion long before we married a year ago. Another leap of faith. And here we are. In our house on my land, which is now also her land.

I look out over our back yard, which isn't fenced off because there's no one around—and Chunkie isn't the kind of dog to stray very far from his home. It's just fields and Texas flatness and ever-changing colors. A good place to raise a child, I think. After all, I was raised in this town, on a ranch only a few miles away, and my family is here. My born-to family and my brand new family.

"Auntie Tess?" I feel Emma's little hand on my arm. I guess I'd better start getting used to interrupted rest and endless questions.

"Yes, darling." I look into Emma's bright young face. She's the spitting image of Megan and, therefore, also of me. For a split second, it feels like looking into the future, and looking into our daughter's face.

"What will you call the baby?" she asks.

The questions are getting more persistent and inquisitive. I glance at Laura and, every time I do, now as much as when we first met, a warmth spreads underneath my skin. We only just decided on a name a few days ago. Laura wanted to start on the design for the birth announcement and she claimed that was impossible without a firm decision on the name.

"Your cousin will be called Milly." After Laura's aunt without whom none of this would have happened, I think. Without whom we wouldn't be sitting here right now, counting the weeks until our child is born.

"That's a pretty name," Emma says. "Mommy says that she and Daddy…" Emma starts chattering again, as much talking to

Chunkie and Socks as to us, and I look over at Laura again. Once we really started thinking about it, coming up with a name was easy. Milly—not short for anything, just Milly— Douglas-Baker will arrive in this house in less than a month's time, and then our lives will start all over again.

Laura never had to say it out loud, but I know that one of the reasons why she wanted to have this child is because of some cosmic awareness that if you take a life, you must create a new one. Perhaps, once Milly is born, she can consider herself even with the universe as well.

As for me, I've felt even with the universe since the day my cart bumped into hers at the supermarket.

"I love you," Laura mouths, and gives the ball of my foot an extra good squeeze.

In response, I give a deep contented sigh, as I smile at my wife and overlook our Texas land.

THE END

ACKNOWLEDGMENTS

Being from Belgium and living in Hong Kong, I've never set foot in Texas, but a certain television show charmed me so much that, after binging on all five seasons twice, I knew I had to set a story in a small town in the great state of Texas. However, I would not have gotten it right without the generous help and input of Texas native and my brand new beta-reader, Carrie. I may have to come visit you in the Lone Star state some day.

As always, I owe a huge debt of gratitude to all of you, my readers. No clichéd saying is more true than the one that says a writer is nothing without her readers. I'm fully aware, dear reader, that without you, I'm nothing. Thank you for making me something.

Cheyenne Blue was once again my trusted guide in the final stages of production of this book. We've worked together on quite a few projects now and her edits, while always on-the-money and precise, hurt me less and less, which leads me to believe that having a friend as an editor is a big advantage. (She also suggested that cowgirl Sherry and best friend Rachel would make a great pairing in another book.)

To all members of my Launch Team: what you do for me and my books is selfless, invaluable, and highly appreciated. (And got me an audio deal!)

Last but by no means least, I must thank my wife, because she's the one who has to deal with all the crazy (and I have a lot of that.) She picks me up when I'm down, does a silly dance for me during our afternoon breaks, and brightens up every single morning simply by waking up beside me.

Thank you.

ABOUT THE AUTHOR

Harper Bliss is the author of the *Pink Bean* series, the *High Rise* series, the *French Kissing* serial and many other lesbian romance titles. She is the co-founder of Ladylit Publishing and My LesFic weekly newsletter.

Harper loves hearing from readers and you can get in touch with her here:

www.harperbliss.com
harperbliss@gmail.com

Made in the USA
Columbia, SC
25 June 2020